LUKE'S TOUCH

NEW YORK TIMES BESTSELLING AUTHOR
LISA RENEE JONES

ISBN-13: 979-8836854478

Copyright © 2022 Julie Patra Publishing/Lisa Renee Jones

All rights reserved. No part of this publication may be reproduced, distributed, or transmitted in any form or by any means, including photocopying, recording, or other electronic or mechanical methods, without the prior written permission of the publisher, except in the case of brief quotations embodied in critical reviews and certain other noncommercial uses permitted by copyright law.

To obtain permission to excerpt portions of the text, please contact the author at lisareneejones.com.

All characters in this book are fiction and figments of the author's imagination.

www.lisareneejones.com

WELCOME READERS!

Writing Luke and Ana was emotional for me. The idea of finding the love of your life and then losing them to a tragedy that feels insurmountable is devastating even in premise. For Luke and Ana, there is history there to draw from, a history that bonds those people together, but obviously, some of that history is painful or they would still be together. Is love enough to bond these two forever when pain and heartache refuse to fade? And in the case of Luke and Ana, will they survive the enemy who wants to kill them long enough to find out?

To begin part two of this journey, I aspire to help you re-enter the world with memories of part one fresh and alive. If you remember, Luke and Ana met at a convenience store that had just been robbed. Ana, an FBI agent, thinks Luke is a bad guy and puts him on his knees, holding a gun on him. Her stepfather, who trains assassins for the government, appears on the scene and knows Luke. He tells her he's a good guy, but no one who is an assassin is a good guy in Ana's mind. But then Luke asks her out and tells her that he lost a friend that week and the idea of kissing her is the only thing that feels good right now.

He wins her over.

And so, the romance begins.

Flash forward a year, and the two are engaged. Luke plans to retire from his overseas contract work after finishing a couple of high-paying jobs that will buy Ana the ranch she dreams of owning. Before that retirement can happen, trouble explodes.

At Ana's bidding, Luke allows her brother, Kasey, to join one of his last missions overseas, which equals a big payday for everyone on his team. The job is to safely transport a princess from one country to another. During this trip, Kasey is secretly running a side mission. Luke catches him handing off a package of some sort to someone at one of the small destination airports. Kasey ends up holding a gun to the head of the princess and long story made very short, Luke is forced to kill Kasey to save the princess and himself.

Meanwhile, Trevor, another one of the men on the assignment, disappears and so does the package. Trevor reappears in the US and beats Luke to Ana to tell her about Kasey's death, which Trevor calls a murder. He claims Luke is the one running dirty side deals and Kasey confronted *him*. There is yet another confrontation, this time between Trevor, Ana, and Luke, and Luke is shot. Luke believes Ana shot him over her brother's murder. In truth, she was certain Trevor was going to kill him, but her gun was knocked out of her hand, and she tried to catch it. It went off and shot Luke. After which, Trevor disappeared, and Luke and Ana fell apart. Supposedly, Trevor died in a car accident several months later.

Flash forward two years after Luke and Ana's breakup, and Luke is working for Walker Security. He still believes Ana shot him. At some point early in their split, he even changed his phone number. She didn't know how to reach him. Now, in the present day, he's on a training drill in Texas with Walker Security, when he gets a call from Jake, a man who'd worked closely with Ana's now-deceased stepfather, and ran a few of his last missions with Luke, including "that" mission. Jake is living in Estes Park, retired, and near his daughter. But retirement is not on his mind now. He's being hunted. He tells Luke there's a hitlist, but before he says more, he's killed. A man grabs Jake's phone and challenges Luke. The basic challenge was: I bet I can get to Ana before you do.

Luke charges to Ana's rescue, finds her, and they have a fiery encounter before they're attacked. Once they are out of the situation and safe, they begin hunting for answers, but nothing between them is right except the sexual tension, which is off the charts. They clearly still love each other. Throughout book one, you work with Ana and Luke to figure out who is on the hitlist, and why. It all comes back to the package. The two of them are on fire the entire time, wanting each other, but fighting the urge until they can't fight it anymore. They're in a safehouse in Breckinridge, Colorado when they make love, talk, and then hit a brick wall about how they get past the fact that Luke killed her brother.

As a side note, Luke's nickname is Lucifer. He's a pilot that flew dangerous missions and took impossible risks. He also did some dirty work for the government. He started to believe he was worthy of the name "Lucifer" until he met Ana. He did confess his past to her, but she already knew him as Luke, a good man. She refused to see him any other way. And therefore, Lucifer started to see himself as Luke as well.

Even now, after he killed her brother, Ana calls him Luke and refuses to see him as Lucifer.

Fast forward, Luke and Ana know they have to put their personal issues aside for now, and focus on staying alive and killing the enemy before the enemy kills them. With that quest in mind, if you remember, Luke suspected that Darius, Ana's longtime friend from the FBI, was dirty, and actually betrayed her and almost got her killed. With Luke and the Walker team's help, Ana seeks to discover the truth. She sets up a meeting with Darius, which he insists be off the grid, behind a corner store. Of course, the location he chooses already sets an ominous tone. Luke doesn't want Ana to go, but Ana is a skilled warrior in her own right, and not about to back down.

She goes to meet Darius.

Luke is hiding a few steps away, behind the wall, and Walker has a team there monitoring the situation. But danger is near, oh so near for Ana. She steps toe to toe with a nervous, anxious version of her friend Darius, but he seems to want to talk. He's about to talk when he is shot dead right in front of her, but not before he sticks a cellphone in her pocket. Luke grabs Ana and the two of them make a run for it. They end up downtown, hiding behind a dumpster when the phone rings. I'm going to start you out by reading the final scene of book one so that we are all back in the moment before book two starts.

And here we go!

I hope you enjoy the journey.

—Lisa

FINAL SCENE OF BOOK ONE

LUCIFER

I push off the dumpster and hold out my hand. "Let me have the phone."

Ana doesn't resist. She hands the cell to me, and I answer the call, already knowing who to expect. The man I spoke to once before. The man who killed Jake. "What do you want?" I ask.

"The package," the man says.

"I don't know what you're talking about."

"And yet, we both know you do. Let. Me. Be. Clear. There are powerful people who want that package. My boss is one of those men. Unless you give it to me in the next twenty-four hours, everyone you have ever known is dead."

My eyes narrow. "I don't have it. I don't know what it is. It must be worth a lot of money for you to be such a drama queen."

"Don't play with me."

"I don't play unless I'm paid. I don't have it, but I'll find it for a price. One million. One week."

It's not what he expects. He's silent a beat that turns into three. That's two too many for him to know what the fuck to do right now. "Two days and I let your people live."

"Then I guess I'll hang up and your very powerful man will kill you for failing him."

"Wait," he says. "Two days and a million dollars."

"A week and two million. I don't know what the fuck it is or where to start looking."

"Five days and one million dollars. And if you go one minute over, I'll kill them all anyway. Don't underestimate me. We're as good as your little Walker team, but we don't play by the rules. Meet me at your little bitch's property, The Ranch. Five days," he repeats. "Don't be late." He disconnects.

If he were as good as he said he is, he'd know his target. He'd know I won't play for pay with the man who killed Jake and threatened Ana. But this works. I bought time to find him and kill him and I will. I hit a few buttons on the phone, text the information on it to Blake, then throw the phone in the trash. That prick won't be contacting me or tracking us. I grab Ana's hand and start running.

CHAPTER ONE

LUKE

"ONLY BY CONFRONTING YOUR INNER DEMONS CAN YOU EVER HOPE TO CONQUER THEM."

—ELLEN HOPKINS

With every step we take about placing critical distance between us and the phone I just chunked in a dumpster, and therefore the enemy hunting us. I hold onto Ana's hand, aware of Darius's blood covering her, just as I am the fact that she was too close to that traitorous prick when he was shot. It could have been her. She could be dead right now, and I'm all kinds of kicking myself for allowing her to meet him and especially behind that damn store. I would die for this woman a million times over and yet I allowed her to risk her life tonight. I didn't find her, save her, and kiss her back into my life to see her die.

What the hell was I thinking?

She might be capable of kicking most men's asses, but she can die as easily as every other flesh and blood human. I should have stood in the way. I should have just tied her to a damn bed, fucked her for twenty-four hours, and let Savage and Adam deal with Darius. If only I could turn back time and erase my stupidity.

Right now, my stupidity aside, I need to get her to safety, but with Darius's blood all over her, we're limited as to where we go until we deal with it. In other words, my first choice—melting into a crowd, where there is safety in numbers, and in the presence of cameras—is not an option. We're left with the path of least resistance—the one that won't have people gaping, favoring the shadows and back alleyways, which is not the fastest, or by far the most public. For now, we're in the business district of downtown Denver, where daytime brings with it the hustle and bustle of evening, and the sunset transforms it into a ghost town.

A place where anyone who moves is an easy target. A place where I once again have to allow her to be a target.

Men like the one who killed Jake and threatened Ana, devour fools who allow themselves to be easy marks. He's going to hope we're fools and send a team in this direction. He's the one acting a fool by thinking for one second I'd work for him. Since I already know he's not a fool, that leaves only one other option. He's a desperate fuck, desperate to please the real boss. Someone is pulling his chain and hard.

Right now, I focus on a homeless man lying on the ground, buried in blankets, seemingly passed out. There's a bottle of water sitting next to him I trade for a twenty-dollar bill and keep walking. A few blocks later, and only when I'm certain we aren't being followed, I lead Ana toward a high-rise building. Once we're there, we shelter behind a concrete wall framing a dock area and another dumpster, illuminated by a street light.

Ana doesn't ask why we stopped here or why I chose this location. She knows and gets busy cleaning up, starting with her jacket. She shrugs out of it and tosses it into the trash, then pulls the beanie from her head, allowing her hair to tumble about her shoulders. The hat is black, a dark shade that hides the blood we both know is there. You don't stand next to a man who takes a bullet and walk away nice and clean.

"How covered am I?" she asks, a weak tremble in her voice that speaks to that human side of her I both fear and love. Darius might have betrayed her, but he was in her life for ten years and she considered him a friend. That feeling of loss and betrayal is an all too familiar blast of emotion I learned even before Ana and I split. It's nothing I ever wanted her to feel, and yet, I know I left. I changed my number. I made her feel those things as well.

Shoving aside emotions neither of us can afford to feel right now, I focus on her question and give her all-black attire a once-over. "Your jacket absorbed most of the noticeable damage." My lips press together. "And your face."

"Of course it did," she says tightly, lifting her chin to present her face for cleanup.

On some level, this moment represents more than necessity. It's about inherent trust and intimacy. It's about us and all the ways we've been bloodied up by the past and the present. I open the bottle of water and pour some on the hat before I start cleaning her up, working to remove the battle scars, as I prefer to think of Darius's blood, right now.

"Was it the same guy who killed Jake on the phone?"

"It was."

"And you promised him what?"

"He threatened to kill people if I don't bring him the package." I toss the bottle and the hat in the trash with her jacket. "I told him I don't give two fucks who he kills and that I only work for money." Some part of me waits for her to believe this is the real me, and damn it, I'm once again transported to the past, to the day I had to tell her I killed Kasey. I'd arrived to her place and Trevor had beaten me there, lying to her, telling her I was dirty, not Kasey. That I was a killer.

"You killed him?" she'd demanded. "You killed Kasey?"

When I'd tried to make her see that I'd had no choice, I'd failed.

"I never understood how love could turn to hate," she'd hissed. "Now I do." She'd moved her hand from behind her back and pressed her gun into my belly. "Why? Why would you do this to me? He was my brother."

But the present plays out nothing like the past. Ana doesn't assume the worst of me. Maybe she never did. Maybe that day we collided in our first moments together since I killed Kasey was nothing but a creation of Trevor and my own guilt because Ana immediately, says, "You were trying to remove the leverage he holds over you."

"That's right," I say. "And he said yes."

"He's desperate," she assumes. "He's not in charge or in control."

"Exactly my thought," I say, but I leave it at that, at least for now.

My sole concern at present is how much blood I just cleaned off of her face. She was standing right there next to Darius when he was shot. She was too fucking close to him for comfort and I let that happen. Aware that there's no way I didn't miss some of the mess on her, I slide out of the lightweight black windbreaker I'm wearing and slip it around her shoulders. She reacts instinctively, all business as she pokes her arms into the sleeves, the material swallowing her hands, and immediately attempts to roll the material.

I take over, quickly adjusting the arm length to wrist level. When her hands are free, and the jacket looks appropriate to her size, I catch her waist under her jacket and lean into her.

"That was too damn close."

"In a number of ways," she agrees, obviously referencing her friendship with Darius. "He was supposed to be my friend."

The way I was supposed to be the one person she counted on above all others. Darius was just one more person to let her down. I won't do that again. "You need to know that I will not let that happen again. I don't care if I make you hate me all over again, I will protect you at all costs. Do you understand me?"

She pulls back, her eyes burning amber in the glint of the dim light. "No," she says tightly. "I *do not* understand. What's your plan? To follow me around and keep me from doing my job? I've worn a badge since before we met, and that's not going to change. You can't protect me. I don't want you to protect me."

"What *do* you want, Ana?"

Her lips press together. "Not to be protected. And too much, apparently. We've been in one place too long. We need to go. Do you understand?"

I want to know what "too much" means, but damn it, she's not wrong. We can't hang out on the street, not if we want to live through the night. "We're not done with this conversation."

"You might not be, but I am." She tries to step out of my grip.

I hold her to me, cup her face, and kiss her hard and fast. "I'm not. I'm not done with anything to do with you. Not now and not ever."

"Okay, that statement contradicts the past two years and makes me angry." She tries to knee me, and I catch her leg. Undeterred, she adds, "And I'm not done with this conversation either."

My lips curving with how easily I drew her into battle, how easily I've always drawn her into battle. It feels like us and I do fucking love us. I want to push her harder. I want to kiss her harder. Instead, I release her and for just a beat we stare at each other, the air ignited with conflict. She turns on her heels and starts walking. I let her go, but not too far. I fall into step beside her. Not behind her. Not in front of her. Beside her, where I forgot to stand.

I won't forget again.

As for her version of too much, there's no such thing, not where Ana is concerned.

If she wants to test me on that, I'm along for the ride.

If she wants to test me on that while naked, even better.

CHAPTER TWO

LUKE

At the top ramp, I scan for trouble and find nothing but empty streets before I say, "We have a bullseye on our backs here. We need the shelter of a crowd. Union Station is a few blocks away and gives us that coverage."

"Agreed," she says, "but should we call your team first?"

"Blake tracks the location of our phones. Right now, we need to get off the streets."

She nods her agreement and we waste no more time on conversation or kisses. We clear the wall, instantly in the open, and I have to hope like hell this asshole we're dealing with knows his package won't matter if he hurts Ana. I'll kill him as fast and nasty as possible and wish I could do it again. Thankfully, for now, no bullets ring out in the night, and no enemies step into our paths.

In a short walk, we arrive at the area I think of as the heartbeat of downtown, which is an entire neighborhood that surrounds the train station. In this area, restaurants, bars, and shopping are easy to find, but we need a place to shelter and connect with our team, which is why I've intentionally brought us up a side street next to a boutique-style hotel. We near it now, and I catch Ana's hand before we round the corner to bring the front entrance into view, the connection blasting a memory through my mind. The first time I'd held her hand just to hold it when I'd never just wanted to hold anyone's hand.

It was that first dinner date. She'd been wearing a pink dress, with glossy lips to match, the FBI agent turned all sweet frilly girl on me and I'd loved the fuck out of the contact. I'd opened her car door and offered her my hand. She'd rotated, and I'd been treated to a view of her long, gorgeous legs. It had taken me all of thirty seconds to fantasize about having them wrapped around my waist. Truth be told, I'd been fantasizing about having her naked since she told me to get on my knees and I wanted her on her knees. In the end, I'm the one who was on a knee for Ana from the moment I met her.

I scan the front valet area to find several cars lined up to unload. Two doormen and two preppy college kids are talking by the bell stand.

No trouble, at least, not as of yet.

Ana and I keep pushing forward, the two of us entering the hotel lobby, only a margin of comfort sliding through me when we are officially off the downtown Denver streets. I drape my arm around her shoulder, as if this is a casual stroll, two lovers returning from an outing, and wish like hell that was the God's honest truth. Ana lifts her chin toward the stairs, and I give an imperceivable nod. Great minds, I think, as that's exactly where I was headed. Away from the common areas, out of the easy view of anyone who enters the hotel hunting for us.

A few long strides and we're climbing to the next level, toward what I believe to be the convention level, which proves an accurate assumption. Once we're on the top level, I scan the carpeted area with chairs in a seating area and hallways left and right.

"Right," she murmurs.

Right it is, I think, guiding her in that direction, but when I would continue on, she tugs me into the

LUKE'S TOUCH

women's bathroom. Once we're inside, I confirm we're in a one-stall number with a lockable door. I lock it while she pees, no shyness in her with me, and that's not just about our history as a couple. She's trained to make necessities a part of her survival, as did I, both of us with her father, who God rest his soul, I still can't help but think, might be attached to this mess. In which case, my opinion of where I'd like his soul to be resting might change.

Wordlessly, Ana washes up, scrubbing her face and hands, checking for wayward blood, washing the death off of her. She says nothing, quiet as a church mouse, but I'm in tune with Ana like no other human on this Earth, and her emotions bang at me like a pot and a metal spoon right by my head.

By the time I've relieved myself as well, Ana is still scrubbing her hands. I slide in next to her, soaping up, aware that I'm the one who cleaned the blood off of her back on the street. There is going to be blood on me too that she doesn't need to see.

She dries her face and hands and I do the same before I step in front of her and catch her hips. "You okay?"

"I'm always okay," she counters, with a defiant lift of her chin that says "I'm Kurt's daughter. How dare you ask me that question," but there is a storm in her eyes, turbulence, and pain that reaches beyond this day and this moment. The past rages between us as a part of the present, a mix of love, hate, and confusion that is stirred with a shot of blood and death.

In other words, translation: no, she is not okay and the more I'm with her, I don't think she has been in a long time. "Right," I say. "Well, at least now we can be 'always okay' together."

"And yet, that didn't prove true at all, now did it?"

"We broke up. I'm back. I'm not going anywhere, Ana."

"And yet, you did."

Memories and emotions pounce on me, a wildcat threatening to tear me open, all over again. "A decision I made when I went to the funeral and you—"

"I know," she says quickly. "*I know* what I did at the funeral."

Memories of me standing behind a tree, and then stepping out of that coverage to allow her to see me, are not kind. Her gaze had lifted and she'd stared at me from a distance, and then she turned and walked away, her hate for everything to do with me crystal clear.

"It was a no-win situation for me," I remind her. "I was the one who—"

"Killed your brother?" she challenges.

"Yes, Ana," I say tightly. "I killed Kasey and if you don't know why now, you never will."

"I know why. I knew then, too, but grief isn't logical. And neither is guilt."

I killed Kasey.

She shot me.

Neither of us understood the whole story about when, why, and how.

No matter what, we have each spent two years feeling betrayed, and hurt. Also, no matter what, I killed her damn brother. You don't come back from that shit. A big part of me knows that despite her claims otherwise, some part of her, even unintentionally, still thinks the worst of me.

This leads me to a shit place right now—her perception of me and the present situation, which is simply put, a double-edged sword laced with love and hate, certain to be the weapon of our demise.

"Is guilt why you tried to contact me, Ana?"

"Guilt is why it took so long."

My jaw clenches. "It's not that simple, is it?"

"I don't remember either one of us gravitating toward anything simple." My cellphone vibrates with a text, and I snake my phone from my pocket to glance at the message from Blake: *I have access to the downtown cameras. I'm sending you a map to follow to get out of your present location and lead you to the car I have waiting for you. Once you can safely do so, call me and keep me in your ear. I'll direct you through any changes in that map based on activity.* The map appears in the message box and I glance at Ana. "Time to get the hell out of here."

CHAPTER THREE

ANA

Luke reaches for the bathroom door and I catch his arm, just the act of touching him, having him right here with me again, unnerving in how natural it feels. It drives home my certainty that I lied to myself and everyone else when I acted as if I was fine without him. I was not fine. I was never going to be fine.

I just felt, as I still do, that no matter what Kasey did, he was my brother, and being with Luke, the man who took his life, was wrong. But it's time to admit to myself that being without him feels just as wrong.

Luke turns to me, a question in his eyes that I quickly answer. "I know, of course, I know, now is not the time for this, but later isn't either if one of us ends up dead. I know I told you I don't know how to be with you, but I really, really don't want you to leave again, either. I just needed to say that."

His eyes burn into mine, seconds ticking by before he pulls me to him, folds me against his warm body, and cups my head. His mouth closes down over mine, his tongue licking long and deep in a stroke I feel in every part of me before he says, "Neither of us is dying tonight. And for the record: you're not okay, as you claimed, or you'd know that without me saying it. You can deny that later. But just so you know, *I am okay.* But I haven't been, not one moment I was away from you. Now let's get the hell out of here."

His words wash away shards of my broken heart, but there are so many broken pieces I fear will never mend, not for me or him. For the moment, I simply hold onto him in every way possible and nod my agreement. He opens the door and captures my hand, and unbidden, when I should be focused on safety first, I'm transported back to our first date. We'd exited the restaurant and he'd caught my fingers in his and then turned me to face him. *"I've never been the hand-holding kind of guy, Ana."*

"But you're holding mine?" I ask, not sure where he was going with this.

"Not because I want to hold you to me. Not because I think you need protection, you've proven you can bring me to my knees," he laughs. I laugh and he adds, *"I just want to. It's the damnedest thing."*

Luke's touch brings me back to the present as he leads me down the stairs toward the lobby, and both of us scan the areas below while my mind draws a familiar realization I'd forgotten until now. I'm not weak without Luke, but I am stronger with him. In the past, when we were side by side, I always knew that whatever war we faced, we'd win together. But then my stepfather died, and Kasey died, and my world was falling apart. I didn't know anything anymore, including myself.

By the time Luke and I are back downstairs in the hotel lobby, Luke has Blake in his ear, verbally guiding us out of this mess. Luke's attention is on Blake and our surroundings, but I don't miss the way he holds onto me a little too tightly. As if he's ready at any moment to take another bullet from me, or rather, for me. Ultimately, everything he did was for me. My brother would never have been with him on that mission had Luke not taken him at my request. Kasey never had his head on straight. Luke was his polar opposite and I'd actually believed that only good things could come from Luke mentoring him.

Luke knew better.
He should have told me no.
God, I wish he would have told me no, but I'd never say that to him. That would be like putting everything on him again. It's not all on him. I knew what Kasey was like. I knew too well, and somehow not enough, which is called blind emotion. I let emotion push everything about how I handled Kasey. And it was ultimately what placed the gun in Luke's hand. I need to say that to him, and so much more.
I'm just not sure it matters.
I think back to a night after we first met, once I'd submitted to the fact that there was no walking away from Luke. I didn't even want to try. We'd had dinner with my family. My father was warm and wonderful to Luke, but Kasey was another story. I flash back to the moment I'd heard my father call him Lucifer, ten times too many.
"Luke," I correct, hitting my limit. "His name is Luke."
My brother snorts. "Like the name erases Lucifer from his blood. You really think if we call him Luke, we erase every reason he earned that nickname?"
"He's a pilot," I start, but Luke squeezes my leg under the table.
"Call me what you want to call me," Luke says. "You're right. A name doesn't define me."
"Doesn't it?" Kasey challenges. "Because from what I've heard, it damn sure does."
Luke's fingers flex on my leg again, but he says nothing. Not a word. Later that night, I want to ask him what my brother had meant. Before I can say anything, Luke does. He walks me to the passenger side of his vehicle and turns to me. "I told you I wasn't like the men your father trains. I didn't lie. I'm worse.

Or I was. I got out of that shit for a reason. And if you want to hear the gritty details, you have a right to hear them. I don't want to tell you." He scrubs his jaw. *"I really don't want to tell you, but I also don't want you to hear it like you did tonight."*

I don't feel shocked or horrified at his confession, which is both raw and vulnerable. And brave, I think. I matter to him or he wouldn't have dared travel this conversational path. I step into him, his hard body aligned with mine, and press my hands to the hard wall of his chest. He is warm. The night is cold. My life was cold without him. "Thank you for your honesty. And tell me when, and if, you're ever ready. I won't listen to anyone else. What you choose to say is all that matters to me." I press to my toes to kiss his cheek.

He scoops up my hair with his fingers, and right there, in front of my stepfather's house, kisses me with the kind of passion that wets a girl between the legs, and has her nipples puckering and tingling.

I'd assumed the best of him that night, and every day forward, at least until Kasey died. Now Luke believes I see nothing but the worst of him. So, while he says he's going nowhere again, I say differently. As we exit the hotel into a chilly night, I fear that trust, or rather our lack of trust, now defines us.

And yet, it doesn't stop him from aspiring, and succeeding, in his recent effort to be my hero. He swooped into my life again, to save me from a similar death to that of Jake. Even now, as we exit the hotel, I don't miss the way he places his body on the side of the road, sandwiching me between him and the wall, sheltering me—ensuring any attack finds him, not me. I never doubted this man's willingness to die for me or even for my brother. I don't know why I questioned anything about the day Kasey died, or why Luke had to kill him. It was grief, I think. Just the freakout mode, of knowing my brother was no longer on this Earth. But if I'm honest, just the idea of Kasey dying at Luke's hand still destroys me, even if logically I know he had no choice but to do what he did.

I told him I don't know how to fix us, and I don't.

The problem is that he doesn't know how to fix us, either.

And no one else can do the fixing for us.

For the moment, I settle on scanning our surroundings and staying alive so we get the chance to try.

CHAPTER FOUR

LUKE

Thanks to the Colorado mountain stream, the wind is an erratic bitch with mood swings, punishing everything in its path, including me and Ana. Compliments of my shared earbuds, Blake barks out commands in both our ears: *left at one street, right at another, left, right. Stop. Stop now. Run East! Run now!*

Neither of us ask any questions. We run and keep running, with Blake back to spitting out commands. Our mad rush ends in a parking lot that's too empty to offer anywhere near a comfortable level of coverage. For now, our best shot at safety is to hunker down at the butt end of an old Buick, but any safety offered is a façade.

"Find a car and get the hell out of there," Blake orders. "Call me when you get to the safe house."

"Copy that, boss," I say, and when he disconnects, I'm already glancing at Ana and patting the rear of the Buick.

She offers an approving nod and sixty seconds later, we're sealed inside the four-door green beast of a car. From there, it takes me another thirty seconds to hotwire the ignition, the clunky chug of the engine far from encouraging.

"She's not going to be fast," I say, "but at least she's a tank if we need to roll over an asshole or two." I hand my phone off to Ana. "The address for the safe house is in my text messages with Blake."

Ana tabs through my phone and quickly offers directions. "211 Monroe Street," she says, and then adds, "If I'm correct, this isn't far from that Italian place we used to love."

I'm instantly reminded of a night not long before that dreaded mission with Kasey when Ana and I had walked down a cozy Cherry Creek sidewalk, her arm linked with mine, her chin tilted upward as she'd offered me a sweet smile. It was a calmer time. We'd been happy together. I'd been happy in a way I'd once thought only flying could make me. Now I'm not. And she's not.

It sends me into a flashback yet again, this time Kasey's funeral, where the smile on her mouth and in her eyes turned to hate, a memory that stabs at my heart, a blade that just won't stop coming. My jaw clenches, anything I might have to say about the past lost in the bloodbath that was our ending. I don't need to go there right now, I tell myself, and yet, as I eye the rearview mirror, finding no cars behind me, the gleam of headlights transports me to a memory from one month after I met Ana—dinner at her stepfather's place.

He'd greeted me at the door and shook my hand. *"You know what I like about you?"* he asks.

"I used to think it was my ability to do my job, sir."

"It still is," he replies. *"And at some point, if my daughter decides you're a keeper, one day, when I'm no longer around, your job will be to protect her."*

This even as Ana grumbles, "I can take care of myself," her stepfather's eyes meet mine, a challenge in their depths, one it doesn't take me long to accept.

I'd met Ana at a time in my life when I had no interest in forever and yet zero ability or desire to walk away from her. Funny how one person can change everything we think we know about ourselves and others. Kurt wasn't a man I expected to invite me into his daughter's life, but he'd done that and more.

Kasey had been a different story, and right out of the gate, he threw darts my way any chance he'd had.

He barely spoke to me, or anyone for that matter, during that first dinner at Kurt's place, casting me condemning scowls. He was going to be a problem, I'd decided then and there. I just didn't know how soon. I didn't know it would be that very night when Kasey and I would have our first confrontation.

I turn us into the residential area of Cherry Creek, where restaurants, shopping, art galleries, and salons are all walkable. At this point, we're a few blocks from the house, and it's time to focus on delivering us to the safe house without any slime slithering along for the ride. The incessant nagging of the past and whatever it's trying to tell me will have to wait.

When I'm certain we haven't been followed, I pull us into the safe house, and thanks to Blake no doubt, the garage door opens automatically, allowing me to pull us inside. Once I've killed the engine, Ana and I sit there in the dark, the air heavy with history, our history as future husband and wife.

I can almost taste our first kiss. I can almost taste her right now. I want to kiss her so damn badly, it's a physical burn.

"When we fuck, we're fucking good," I say. "When we're not, we used to be just as good. Since we've both agreed we can't fix what's broken, we might as well just get naked and fuck like rabbits." I glance over at her.

"That's your answer to our problems? Just get naked and fuck?"

"Right now? Yes, it is."

As if the universe wants to fuck over my plan to fuck, my cellphone rings and we both know I can't ignore it the way I'd like to ignore our problems.

CHAPTER FIVE

LUKE

I don't even bother to eye the caller ID. I know it's Blake. "Yeah, boss," I say, answering on speaker. "You've got me and Ana."

"Parker never showed up at the airport. We can't reach him."

Parker was one of the men working with me that night in Egypt when I was forced to kill Kasey. They went after him, too, but unlike Jake, he got away alive.

My fingers curl on the steering wheel with this news.

He was a good man.

"He wouldn't no-show," I say tightly. "He was either forced to go off the radar or he's dead, most likely dead. Where are Adam and Savage?"

"They're following a vehicle I captured on the street feed. What do I need to know on your end?"

"Darius dropped a phone in Ana's pocket. When it rang, I answered. It was the same bastard who killed Jake. He wants the package. I told him I want a payday. He was desperate enough to buy my story. Obviously, he's beholden to someone he doesn't want to disappoint. He gave me five days. The interesting part of this story, though, is where he wanted to meet up. He chose Ana's property. Anyone who knows Ana's father and the facility she inherited knows it's booby-trapped out the ass."

"Unless they were close enough to the family to know the traps," Blake suggests. "Who would that be, Ana?"

"No one comes to mind," she says, "but I also don't know who my brother might have let in on the family secrets."

Trevor, I think, considering he and Kasey were the ones running the dirty job behind my back. "Any word on Trevor's present state of life or death, Blake?"

"As soon as you two stop getting in fucking trouble, I'll finish looking for him. On that note, go rest. We're now operating on a clock. By my estimation, we have four days and twenty-three hours until D-day." He disconnects.

I reach for the door. Ana catches my arm, her touch burning through me, my cock instantly hard. I'm on edge and I know myself well enough to know I need to come down. I need an outlet. Just that fast, I want to pull her to me, to feel her warm and wet body squeezing my cock, right here in the car. I'm about to make it happen, to yank her across my lap, when she asks, "You think Parker is dead?"

Fuck. We're having this conversation. "He's dead."

"How does that help them find the package?"

"It reminds me that if I don't deliver the package, more people die." My lips press together, my nerves ticking with a mix of anger and self-blame I was working real fucking hard to escape a few seconds ago. Now I'm swimming in all kinds of bullshit.

I told the men who worked for me that the jobs we took were safe. Ana trusted me to bring Kasey home. I failed on all counts. Suffocating in my own emotions, I open the door, exiting the car.

Ana is out before I can round the car, joining me at the door. I open it and allow her to enter first. She hesitates, studying me, and I feel the push of words she wants to speak but bites back. Does she want to call me a killer? Maybe she won't say it, but I know she's had that thought. She enters the house. I follow her down a small hallway and into a kitchen with a connected living room.

The place is nice, I guess, modern, with a giant white island and a whole lot of navy blue everywhere. Not that I give two fucks about décor right now or ever. Ana takes it all in beside me for about thirty seconds and then turns to face me. "You were deep ops," she says, her segue to logic I'm never going to hear right now. "Easy jobs or not, the work comes with risks and they all knew the risks, including me. You know you didn't get Parker or anyone else killed."

She's wrong, but she doesn't want to hear that right now, and I'm not in the mood to have her dogmatic desire to win this battle. Because she won't. Then we won't. And I'm pretty damn tired of us losing together.

I reach for her, pull her into me, mold her close, and despite everything hard and harsh about this night, she is a soft, heady mix of past and present that both torments and soothes in one hot minute. My cock is hard, pressing against my zipper, my body tense with the adrenaline rush of wanting her like I never wanted anyone but Ana. But then, me craving her, everything about her with all-consuming need is nothing new, nor is it anything I've ever attempted to resist. That's another battle with Ana I'd lose but do so happily. This, her and I naked and wild for each other, won't erase the pain or anger of the past, or even my guilt about the men we've lost, but it damn sure offers a really fucking amazing outlet.

My hand frames her jaw and tilts her head back to look at me, but I don't reply to her words. Kissing her makes a whole hell of a lot more sense. Her breath is warm, her lips tempting, and I savor how familiar and right this feels, no matter how much our history tells me it's wrong.

I lower my mouth to hers, a prelude to getting her naked, which is where I do my best talking.

"Kissing me won't end this conversation," she promises.

"It will," I assure her. "It abso-fucking-lutely will. At least until we get our clothes back on."

With that, my mouth closes down on hers in a kiss meant to seduce her and drug me in the way only Ana can.

CHAPTER SIX

ANA

When I was a little girl, before my mother died, she used to bake chocolate chip cookies. I was allowed one per night after dinner, but I was addicted, and naughty me, would sneak out of my room and steal a cookie. I'd hunker down by the kitchen island, out of the sight of the door, and nibble away.

My behavior was oh so bad, but the cookie was oh so good.

That's how I feel about Luke.

Addicted.

Naughty.

Oh so right, and somehow oh so wrong.

I could demand we make the wrong right by talking through the past, by talking about why he can't even share a memory of a restaurant with me. The problem is we are more complicated than those minor topics.

Parker is dead.

His guilt is alive.

I helped create his self-blame with how I handled Kasey's death.

I'm back to we should talk, but his kiss—*God*, his kiss—undoes me, destroys my objections. How can it not? His hands are under his coat I'm still wearing and he's all over me, my senses on fire with his touch. The truth is that I didn't think I'd ever feel him touch me again. I didn't want anyone else. I never got over him. I never even tried.

And the truth is, the physical side of our renewed connection is far easier to navigate than the emotional side. In other words, I want just what he wants right now. To drown out everything else, to forget about the blood that was all over me, the death that clings to the night and our lives.

I lean into him, press my body against his hard, hot body, the feel of him next to me, weakening my knees, and awakening nerve endings. I'm tingling all over, wet and wanting, my breasts heavy, my nipples puckered little balls. His lips part mine, lingering a breath from another kiss, the taste of him alive on my tongue, a heady mix of dominance and desire that speaks to me and overwhelms me in every possible way.

He wants to fuck me now. I know because I know him, because I feel the same, because in those lusty moments the things that divide us disappear, if only for a short while. When we are naked and he's pressing me for more this or more that, pressing me even beyond my comfort zone, he's asking for trust.

He doesn't understand that trust was never the issue.

Heartache and loss were, and when those two monsters bare their teeth, they always bite, and do so fiercely and with an intensity felt to the soul. They aim to latch onto everything you hold dear and gnaw at it until there is nothing left but a skeleton of what once existed.

But no monster could destroy what I feel for Luke, and while it hurts that he thinks otherwise, I also know I deserve that doubt. So, if he needs to push me, to test me, to try to understand who I am with him and who he is with me, I'm all in.

He drags the jacket, his jacket, down my arms, his teeth scraping my bottom lip, that raw primal side of Luke I know all too well is present right now. This is the side of Luke that knew nothing but death when he met

me. He lost his parents. He lost everyone close to him when he was serving his country. And those losses created the side of him that shut down emotionally, to the point that his duty included doing what others could not. He took risks when he flew, killed when he had to kill, and dared anyone to tell him he couldn't do whatever the hell he needed to do to get his job done.
He saw blood and death.
He created blood and death.
And then he met me.
Suddenly he was awake emotionally again and that wasn't easy for Luke. Because you can't choose to wake up and feel only some things and not others. And he was wide awake when he shot Kasey. He has dealt with that alone.

Guilt stabs at me, a sword that he knows all too well, and I can't bear the idea of hiding from my role in that truth. I tear my mouth from his, my fingers digging into his arms. "Luke—"

"You of all people should be calling me Lucifer, Ana," he says, his hands settling on my arms, his touch warm on my skin. I missed this man's hands on my body far too much to believe I made it without him.

"Only when you're naked and teasing me."

He doesn't need further encouragement, not when he's like this. By the time I've tossed it away, he's dragging the front of my top down, taking my bra with it. His eyes rake over my breasts, his fingers catching my nipples. My sex clenches, dampness pooling slick and hot between my thighs.

He scoops my backside and gives it a squeeze. "Damn, your ass is perfect." His fingers slide low and reach intimately, teasing my sex. "And you're so fucking wet."

I don't know why, but I suddenly want him to come back from this dark place. I want him to talk to me. "We're avoiding—"

"Nothing," he assures me. "I'm avoiding *nothing*."

I'd reject his words as surely as I would his claim that he's never going to leave again, but there is a raw, tormented quality to his voice that reminds me that he's in that dark place in his head. The place that doesn't listen to reason because it doesn't come from a place of reason. It's about emotions, about his past and now our past, about everything bad that has ever stolen what he thinks is the good in his life.

That's when I realize I'm the one who stole all that was good in his life, at least in his mind. And that's when I realize just how much Luke hates me.

CHAPTER SEVEN

ANA

I want to tell Luke that nothing and no one took me away but him. Actually, I want to shout it at him, scream it at him, beat it into him with words he actually hears. He left. He made that choice. Just as he can choose to stay again. But it's not that easy, I know it's not that easy, not after what happened with Kasey. The impossibility of it all is what he feels and it's spiraling inside me now, deep inside me, down to my broken heart and tormented soul.

And besides, I pushed him away at first. That's why he left. That's why he cut me off.

I'm angry with him. I want to punish him. I want to comfort him. I just plain want him, and I don't know where to put those emotions any more than he does.

Luke's gaze meets mine and I can feel the push of his probing stare, his desire to crawl inside my mind and read my thoughts. And yes, I can feel his anger, familiar and ripe, the way it was when I met him. He hid it beneath his burn for sex, his burn to push me, his need for me to trust him more than he trusted himself.

Because if I could trust him, maybe he could again, too. If we were somewhere else, alone, and without the pressure of a hitlist, with his Walker crew joining us, I know I'd be every which way with this man, as he pushed me, tested me, even tied me to a bed. He'd be tormenting me until he knew I trusted him again.

But we're here, and we can't escape those things. Time presses on us while the burn between us is scorching the very air we breathe.

Suddenly, the barriers between us are gone, wiped away, the war between us set aside, even if only in the darkness of our pain. His mouth crashes down on mine, and I taste the wildness in him, the hunger. I taste a man who knows only one thing. What he wants. And right now, that's me.

It's a contagious kind of feeling that has me tugging at his clothes with no reward. He's in control when he's like this, a little detail I learned I like far more than I expected when I first saw this side of him. Until that night, only a month into our relationship, he'd made love to me. But he was a man with darker needs, and once he properly fucked me, I wanted more. Like I want more now.

Luke's fingers hook in the elastic of my baggy sweats, his palms pressing beneath, as he skims them down my legs, kneeling in front of me and Lord help me, he licks my clit. Tormenting me because he is not going to slow down enough to finish what he started. I'm right, of course. He cups my hips on either side and kisses my belly, but then he's standing, his eyes raking over my naked breasts as he unzips himself and frees the jut of his rock-hard erection.

My nipples are puckered, my mouth is dry while my sex is slick, my thighs wet with my arousal. He steps to me, tangles rough fingers in my hair, and drags my mouth to his, kissing me even as he cups my ass and lifts me, sitting me on the edge of the counter. He presses my legs open, his hand sliding between my legs, his fingers testing me, sliding inside me. He groans, and that's it. That's all the wait he has in him. His hand presses to my thigh, and he impatiently brings me closer, a firm grip on his cock as he slides it along my sex. He presses into the wet heat of my aching body and then enters me, impossibly slow at first, until he's there, all the way buried to my core.

And when he would normally go wild right then and there, he cups my face and drags my gaze to his. "You have no idea how much I missed being inside you."

My teeth scrape my bottom lip at the intimate, erotic confession.

And for just a moment, there is only us and it's as if we are a puzzle that is no longer missing pieces. We are those pieces. Luke lowers his mouth, his breath warm, lingering there a moment before he kisses me. It starts as a slow, luscious slide of his tongue and becomes a ravenous demand.

Control belongs to our bodies now.

My arms wrap around his neck and he drives into me, but the angle is off and he growls in frustration. Undeterred, he cups my backside and lifts me, holding my weight.

He thrusts and pulls me into him, several slow sultry sways of our bodies, a flame to fire yet to consume us. Luke's hand slides between my shoulder blades, his cheek to my cheek as he whispers, "Lay back."

It's not a command no matter who it's been spoken to. It's a question, one I suspect he will ask me in every erotic way possible. Will I trust him to hold me and not let me fall, a question that is bigger than the physical moment. I don't know if I trust him not to leave, but this man raced across a state line to save my life. I trust him. I trust him more than anyone else in my life now or in the past.

My hands slide away from his neck and I ease back. His eyes gleam with satisfaction as he grips my waist, holding me up as he thrusts into me. My breasts are between us, ripe for his viewing, swaying and bouncing with every move. But it is him who mesmerizes and arouses me. His powerful body, his intense expression.

The rub of his thick erection moves along my nerve endings, pumping, and thrusting, and I am over the edge. I curl my fingers on his arm. "Luke," I whisper, with the tensing of my body, the promise of magic soon to follow. "Luke, I—"

He folds me forward against him, my naked breasts against his naked chest, rocking with me, a little move that always takes me over the edge. And it does. That's how well his body still knows my body. I quake in his arms, my sex clenching around him, and he groans with the impact. He quakes, his face buried in my neck, a low guttural sound sliding from his lips. A few seconds later, he sets me on the counter, holding onto me. We don't move. I don't want to. I don't think he does, either.

CHAPTER EIGHT

ANA

I find myself holding onto Luke the way I wish I would have held onto him in the past, my fingers flexing against the taut muscles in his shoulders, but unbidden, my mind now as alive as my body. And I'm not thinking about the hot encounter we just shared, as I wish I were, but rather how Luke's reaction to Parker's disappearance led to me half naked to my present state of undress on top of a random kitchen island.

If the past two years have taught me anything it's that silence isn't always kinder or sweeter than conversation.

"You didn't get Parker killed," I say again. "This isn't your fault." When his hand settles on my side, his fingers gentle where they rest at my waist, I'm encouraged enough to add, "You aren't responsible for Kasey's death. Kasey made that happen. I know that, Luke. I need you to know that, too."

He noticeably tenses, and before I can stop it from happening, he pulls out of me, lifts me, and sets me on the ground before handing me a roll of paper towels. His eyes meet mine, anger burning in their depths. "And yet you don't know how to be with me anymore."

"Luke," I whisper, but it's too late. I've gone too far, too soon, by treading into the Kasey territory. He's shut down and shut me out, proven by the fact that he steps backward, placing space between us and offering me his back as he rights his pants. I'm still standing there in shock when his hands settle on his hips, and his gaze lifts upward. "Get dressed, Ana," he orders softly.

His words hit me like an emotional slap when I'm quite certain Luke has digested my words with the same impact, and I don't know how to fix this or us. That was the point I was trying to make to him in the shower yesterday. I don't know how to fix two years of emotions on either side.

Especially not right here and now.

I grab my pants and walk around the island, doing what I have to in order to put myself back together.

Luke snatches up his shirt, and still facing the other way, pulls it over his head, ripples of tense muscle flexing all the way down his upper torso. I walk about to the end of the island and almost as if he's timed it as such, the moment I find my position there again, he turns to face me. "Luke, I know you couldn't control Kasey. I know you didn't intend to kill him. I know you had no other choice."

"If you knew Kasey's death wasn't my fault, you wouldn't have such a hard fucking time figuring out how to be with me, Ana."

A pinch in my chest becomes a blast of adrenaline and emotion, my voice lifting with my reply, my hand cutting through the air. "You forget there's more to this than one emotional night. You left me, Luke, you, my ride or die, *left me*. I spent two years dealing with this alone, and while I know you did the same, I didn't make that decision."

"You pushed me away."

"I was emotional and hurt." The reply rasps through clenched teeth. "I didn't need you to leave. I needed you to hold on tighter. That's what married people do. They hold on tighter."

"We weren't married, Ana."

I can almost feel the color drain from my face. "No," I croak out, hugging myself against the blow he's just

44

delivered. "No, we weren't. How did I forget that? And I have your ring locked away safely to do with what you want." I rotate with the intent of escaping.

He's there quickly, catching my arm, turning me to him, his touch both fire and ice somehow heating my skin and still chilling me inside and out. "You took that wrong," he murmurs. "You didn't want to marry me," he claims.

"Says you, not me," I reply, my tone softer now, the energy to yell or shout drained out of me, but I have the misfortune of still feeling too much where Luke is concerned. Just *too much*.

"Ana," he says, his tone gentler now, rough with emotion, the deep baritone of his voice doing funny things to my belly, stirring a reaction to him that is all about heat and love.

He steps a little closer and I tell myself to back up, to move away, to run away before he cuts what's left of my heart into pieces and watches me bleed out.

His cellphone rings and he grimaces, cursing under his breath. "I have to take this."

"I know," I say, "and maybe that's for the best anyway."

A muscle in his jaw ticks and he releases me, reaching for his phone. It buzzes with a text message that he reads before glancing at me. "Savage and Adam just pulled into the garage."

"I really need to wash the death off me anyway. I'll leave you to them." I turn away.

"Ana," he says, his voice a firm demand that I halt.

I do, but it's a mere pause without a turn. I glance over my shoulder. "Yes?"

"We're not done talking."

"I think we should be, Luke. I think I am."

It's at that moment the door opens and I turn away, rushing toward the staircase, eager to be anywhere but in this room with Luke. And yet, I've spent the past two years wanting to be anywhere I could find Luke.

CHAPTER NINE

LUKE

Footsteps sound behind me and I curse at the poorly timed interruption, turning with the expectation that I'll be joined by Savage and Adam, only to watch Parker walk in the door. Big, broad, and tall, with sandy brown hair and a love for leather jackets, he walks toward me, hands out to his side. "Mr. Beautiful is here. Did you miss me?"

Relief washes over me and I meet him step by step, pulling the bastard into a bear hug. "I thought you were dead."

He laughs and pulls back giving my shoulder a playful nudge. "Give me some damn credit, man. I've got skills and they're multiplying, but I'm not losing control. I can't fly a plane. I was stuck with some private pilot who was afraid of a little lightning."

"Pussy," I murmur jokingly. "You should have flown the damn thing yourself."

"Then I would be dead." His smile fades, his mood sobering. "How many of us are dead?"

"Jake so far. Executed and used for bait."

"Ana?"

"She's here."

He scrubs his jaw. "Thank you, Lord, for that. I need a motherfucking drink." He walks past me into the kitchen, opens the empty fridge, and slams it shut. "Or not." He turns to face me. "What do you know?"

"First, where the hell are Savage and Adam?"

"They dropped me off and went to the store."

In other words, nothing came from any lead they followed tonight, and Savage is—as Savage always is—hungry. I meet Parker on the other side of the island, on a mission for answers. I trust Adam and Savage and there was a point when I trusted Parker, but when trouble brews and originates from the past, no one from that era instantly earns anything but my caution. "What do *you* know about Trevor?"

He doesn't even blink. "Besides him being a dirty bastard when he was living? He's dead and we're all better for it."

"How do you know he was dirty?"

"We all knew what happened on that mission. That and I stayed in touch with Jake."

"When?" I ask because this relationship is news to me. Parker wasn't one of Kurt's men. He was one of mine. He served with me. And he never worked with Jake before that dreaded day. He served with me. "And how did you get close to Jake?"

"We had a drink after Kasey's funeral. He was a mess. I ended up hanging out with him for a few days. As for when he told me about Trevor, he texted me right after his accident. I ditched my phone, but it's in my call log."

Something Blake can check and I'll damn sure make sure he does. "When was the last time you talked to Jake?" I ask.

"About six months ago. We connected around the holidays. He was always trying to get me to come spend them with him."

As he did me, I think. Jake had my number and Ana did not. I shove away that thought that goes nowhere pretty. Ana should have known how to reach me in an emergency. That she didn't is on me and shitty.

As for why Jake took to Parker, he liked orphan types, and Parker literally is an orphan. He grew up in a children's home, a man with no family, his loner status one that made him a wicked soldier, risk-taker, and killer when necessary. It's the kind of empty man scenario that either makes a man right or wrong, depending on the man. Jake believes it made Parker devoted to our team, which was our family at the time.

Jake was never wrong about people.

And yet, he's dead, and whoever killed him knew how to get past his many precautions. Sounds like Jake kept that kind of connection to Parker. "Did you ever go out to his place?" I ask.

His lips press together, regret flitting through his eyes before he says, "No. I spent my last holiday buried in a redhead. I figured there was always this year. I regret that decision right about now. What I won't regret is killing whoever killed Jake. So, when you're done turning me into a suspect, let me know. I'm in for the kill."

There's the Parker I know. A man who was always direct and in for the kill. A man I trusted. I never trusted Kasey or Trevor, both of whom Kurt pushed me to hire. And then there is the film of the attack at Parker's home. There is no doubt they came for him, just as they did Jake and Ana.

"The dickhead ring leader of these assholes made contact. He wants the package."

"The package? You mean whatever the hell it was Kasey and Trevor were trying to hand off in Egypt?"

"Seems that way."

"Two years later? Why now?"

"You tell me. What do you know?" I repeat.

"How to stay the hell out of trouble which brings me back to this hitlist and why now, why two years later?

What are we supposed to know that I don't know? And what does this have to do with Trevor dying? Was that a hit?"

"I don't believe for a minute that car accident was a hit. I'm not sure I believe Trevor's dead. The package disappeared with him."

"Two years ago," he repeats. "We're swimming in circles. Was Jake tortured? Did they think he had the package? And if these assholes think we have the package, why didn't they come for us sooner?"

Was Jake tortured?

It's a good question that leads to places I haven't fully considered. "No," I say. "Jake wasn't tortured, but his pregnant daughter slept a few miles away. It's possible they threatened her."

"And in the end, was she tortured?"

"No," I say, which actually doesn't quite add up if these assholes really thought Jake knew where the package was. They'd use his daughter to get him to talk, the way they tried to get Ana to use me to talk."

"Was his daughter killed?"

"No," I reply.

"That leaves us with only one of two assumptions," he replies. "Jake knew where the package was, told these assholes, and they killed him so he wouldn't be around to talk to anyone else."

"No," I say. "They think I have the package. And as we stand here talking, I don't think they ever thought Jake had it."

"Then why go after him?"

"To make sure I knew they'd kill Ana if I didn't cooperate."

Because somehow, some way, all of this is about her.

LUKE'S TOUCH

It's not a logical thought when these assholes seem to be after me, but my gut says it's true, and my gut never lies to me.

CHAPTER TEN

LUKE

Parker arches his brow. "Why do they think you have the package?"

"I have no fucking clue," I say, "but my gut says Trevor's involved."

"I thought he was dead?"

"What if he's not?"

His brows furrow. "It takes money to fake that shit, but then, everyone who worked for you made boatloads. I mean, why the hell did Kasey or Trevor need to run a side gig in the first place?"

Because Kurt was in financial ruin, I decide, which I assume now based on how he handled his will, but logically, based on what I know of his business, makes no sense. But I've also got to open my mind to possibilities. What happened to Kurt's money?

My mind travels back to that first dinner at Kurt's place once again, but beyond this time, to the confrontation with Kasey that followed.

After Ana and I leave and go back to her place to stay the night, I run to the store to replenish her Diet Sprite for her before we start a movie. I see the headlights in my rearview, an uneasy feeling in my belly. I test them, turning in an unplanned direction down a dirt road, then cutting right down yet another dirt road.

I made enemies in the military, as has everyone on my team, running missions only a handful of officials knew we ran. The only thing I can think of is Ana. Is she safe? Are they going after her? But I also can't lead them to her. That means I have to deal with my problem, which means whoever owns those headlights.

I whip down a dirt road to the right, do a quick U-turn, and meet the asshole head-on. By the time he skids to a halt, I have a Glock in my hand, and I'm walking toward him. It takes me about thirty seconds to figure out it's Kasey in hulk formation and charging toward me, no gun in obvious sight. I shove mine in my pants at my back and meet him toe to toe.

"What the hell are you doing, Kasey?"

He pops my jaw with a mighty blow I feel pretty damn well and good. I grimace with the pain—and shake it off and smile. "Now can I get your sister her Diet Sprites? She gets really cranky without her Diet Sprite."

"I don't like you," he pretty much growls at me.

"I would never have guessed."

"You cocky prick."

"What's your real problem here?"

"I don't trust you."

"What did you want to happen tonight? What do you want now?"

"I was just keeping an eye on you. You turned it into this."

My cellphone rings in my pocket. "That's going to be Ana."

I grab my phone and answer. "Hey, baby. Sorry, I'm taking so long. I just ran into your brother. We're chatting. I'll be there soon."

"Oh no," she murmurs. "I know he's difficult, but I love him. Please try to tolerate him."

"For you," I say. "Just for you."

I disconnect. "Anything else, Kasey?"

LUKE'S TOUCH

He glares at me and rotates on his heel, marching toward his truck.

When I get back to Ana's place, she greets me at the door in a tank top and shorts, takes one look at the swelling of my face, and freaks. "Oh my God, what happened?" she worries.

I scoop her into my arms. "Nothing you can't kiss and make better." Our next stop is her bed.

So, where does this memory lead me, and why is my head in this space?

Why indeed, I think.

The answer comes to me easily, a seed in my mind that has finally formed roots.

Some people keep their enemies at a distance. Some keep them close and easily reached. After that first confrontation with Kasey, I knew I was his enemy, but what if I was Kurt's as well? And why? It's a crazy thought. I never had a problem with Kurt, but maybe I knew something I didn't know I knew?

What the hell would that be, though?

And if so, if I represented some kind of threat, why was he okay with me being in his daughter's life?

Also, in the end, why did Kurt leave Kasey with expenses he couldn't pay unless he worked for me? I'm supposed to believe that was to teach Kasey to hustle, at the expense of Kurt's empire failing if his son failed. That doesn't add up to me.

I'm not sure the package is where this story started.

CHAPTER ELEVEN

LUKE

"Why now?" Parker presses again, drawing me out of my speculation about Kurt's financial woes.

"They, whoever *they* are, must have thought the package was in one set of hands, an unattainable set of hands. Until someone tried to unload it, which set off some sort of alert."

"Trevor," he assumes. "Now I see where you're going with this."

The garage door alert goes off again and I can instantly hear Savage running his mouth. "And then she said, fuck you and your billy goat, but I didn't laugh. Who has a billy goat?"

Parker arches a brow. "Savage runs his mouth in all kinds of directions," I explain. "You get used to it and him."

Savage and Adam appear in the kitchen. "Better running my mouth than running around like a chicken with my head cut off," Savage says, walking toward the fridge.

Adam stops at the end of the island and sets a couple of bags on top, sliding one of them in front of me. "I thought Ana might need a change of clothes. We did the best two guys and no help can do."

Savage joins us and sets a six-pack on the island before producing a bottle of whiskey and sliding it in my direction. "I thought Ana might need this after watching her partner get splattered all over her tonight. Unless you're as cold as me, that shit gets to you."

He's not wrong.

Ana is a ball of torment layered on top of more torment, and it's about to get worse, considering this conversation with Parker has led me down a jagged path I don't want to travel and one she will not as well. One that leads to her father. I don't believe he's alive, but then again, his body never made it home. He's involved in this, even if it's from the grave. I can't prove it, but I also can't wait until I can talk to Ana, not when we're on the run and I'm trying to keep her alive.

She knows things she might not even know she knows.

It's our job together to figure out what those things might be.

I glance at Adam. "Tell Blake to look up Ana's stepfather and dig into his final affairs, in every context possible. Kasey was working because Kasey had to work. Because Kurt left him with bills and not enough resources to cover those bills."

"Kurt was dead when we ran that mission," Parker points out.

"So is Trevor supposedly," I reply, "but the worst kind of dead is the kind still walking around and taking shots at you from behind."

"Are you saying Kurt's alive?" Parker asks.

"At least in the sense that he has more to do with all of this than I realized at first." I grab the bottle and meet Adam's stare. "I need to go bring Ana up to speed. What's our plan?"

"I hear you made a five-day deal," he replies. "So, I think I should be the one asking you what's the plan."

"To kill these motherfuckers, which I'll enjoy more with some sleep."

"Eat, sleep, kill, eat," Savage chimes in. "Sounds like a movie title I can get into."

Adam gives a short nod. "Agreed."

Parker is more of the same. "No complaints here."

I snap up the bag of clothes and start walking, dreading the conversation I have to have with Ana now rather than later. She's angry at me for walking away. She's angry at me for killing Kasey. Now I have to go after her stepfather. It's almost as if I want her to hate me because if she didn't already, she might before this night is over.

CHAPTER TWELVE

LUKE

"*That's what married people do. They hold on tighter.*"

I climb the stairs to the second level of the house, seeking out Ana and kicking myself for how I replied to those words. *We aren't married, Ana.* Holy mother of God, what was I thinking? It came off like a rejection when I wanted her to be my wife, the only woman I would ever marry. The only woman I will ever love. Obviously, that wasn't her point. We both know we're not married. We both know we were engaged with every intention of being married, which requires the same commitment as marriage itself.

Meanwhile, I've been dragging her to me and kissing her, holding onto her in the physical, and then making ridiculous statements like that one. I must have her confused as hell.

And I fear I'm about to make it worse.

I don't just have to take her back to the past that destroyed us, I have to question the morality of everyone she called family but me.

Reaching the top of the landing, I cut right to find a closed door I assume tells me where Ana is right now, the primary bedroom with an attached bath. I approach and I can hear her voice in my head. *You left me, Luke, you, my ride or die, left me.* That statement bleeds with remnants of her past. Everyone has left her; her mother, her father, her brother, they all died. Then me. I left, the one person who swore I'd never leave. I'd thought it was what she wanted, and that decision will now haunt me from this point forward.

I left her to grieve alone.

I left her to live alone.

For better or worse means for better or worse. I didn't ask her to be my wife because I planned for everything in life between us to be roses. Of course, she tried to push me away. Of that, there is no question, but even if it was subconsciously, on some level she needed to know I'd stay anyway. I failed her. And I failed us.

And just like that, I'm standing outside the bedroom door, but I'm living that last night in Breckenridge, reliving my time with Ana there. I'm sitting in the chair in a bedroom, in the minutes right after we'd had sex, after we'd seemed to tear down walls, and start building them stronger.

The shower turns on, which feels like avoidance. No. Not happening. She will not hide from me. I stand up and I don't bother with my clothes. Sure enough, I find her in the shower. I open the door and join her, pulling her to me.

"What's going on?"

"Nothing." *She folds her arms in front of her, almost shyly. Ana is not shy.* "I just needed the hot water," *she adds.*

"What's going on?" *I repeat, guiding her out of the flow of water and against the wall.*

"I'm fine."

"You're not fine," *I insist.*

"Wasn't there another way?" *she blurts, her voice trembling with emotion.* "Couldn't you have shot his leg or his arm?"

My hands fall away from her. "He had a gun to the head of the princess I was escorting to another country. He'd killed three of our men. And I had no *idea who was left that was on my side. No. It was him or me and the princess, and she was an innocent, Ana."*

She squeezes her eyes shut. "I don't know how to do this, Luke." She opens her eyes. "I don't know how to be without you, but I don't know how to be with you, either. It feels wrong. You killed Kasey."

But it's more than that, I think, returning to the present.

I killed Kasey and then I left her to deal with the pain alone.

Damn it, I have to just deal with the trouble we're in and then talk to her about us. I knock on the door, only to find the door is actually cracked. I know Ana, and this is her way of saying, if it's necessary, come in, even if she'd prefer I not. It doesn't mean she wants me or us. It's about logic and her training again, her understanding that right now, we're on the run and emotions don't get to dictate her decisions. Obstacles, like locked doors, can save, or cost, a life.

I step into the room to find a bed as the centerpiece while two chairs sit to the right by the window. Ana is nowhere in sight, but her shoes are at the end of the mattress, and the shower is running in the connected bathroom, with the door half-open.

With a lift of my hand, I toss the bag of clothes on the bed and open the bottle of whiskey, slugging back a drink, the burn of the booze far more welcome than the burn of my actions. I carry the bottle with me and step into the bathroom, and halt when I find Ana standing in a glass-encased shower, water flowing over her face, her perky little bottom facing me. It's perfect, and I know just how it feels in my hands and pressed against my cock, a cock that is presently attempting to salute her banging, beautiful body.

Ana turns off the water, taking her time to wring the water from her long hair before allowing it to rest just above her narrow waist. I'm imagining my hands on her waist, pulling her down on top of my rock-hard cock, when she reaches for her towel. I want to deny her that towel, and join her, fuck her, make love to her, but there is too much wrong between us to make that right.

Damn it to hell.

I'm about two seconds from closing the space between us and getting naked with her when I realize this needs to be on her terms as much as possible. Our breakup was on my terms. Our recovery has to be on hers. For this reason, I force myself to lean on the bathroom counter and just wait, wait until she's ready for me. At this point, she hasn't noticed me yet, which tells me it's a good decision. She is not herself right now, but then, she just saw Darius, another long-term presence in her life, die. And once again, I cut her off.

Fuck me, because I just keep fucking her and not in a good way.

It's not until she's wrapped her hair and then twined a towel around her lush curves, that she steps out of the shower and gasps as she brings me into view.

"Luke," she whispers, her body tensing.

Not the reaction I want from the woman I love.

I lift the bottle of whiskey in the air. "I brought you a little liquid relaxation."

"I'm not sure dulling my senses is what either of us needs to do right now."

If we were about to fuck, I'd agree, I think, but we have to talk, and it won't be an easy conversation to digest for either of us. "We're not going anywhere until we get a good night's sleep," I counter, shaking the bottle in her direction, hoping to lure her a little closer and acutely aware of the fact that all that stands

LUKE'S TOUCH

between me and her is space and that little terry cloth towel.

CHAPTER THIRTEEN

LUKE

Ana dries her hair and tosses the towel she used to do so away, securing the one around her body a bit more firmly before she moves to stand in front of me. There's a droplet of water on her lips, and my tongue longs to lick it away. I don't have to see beneath the terry cloth to know she's cold, to know her nipples are puckered and ripe for my mouth to warm them up.

She grabs the bottle and slugs back a drink, grimacing with the bite of the alcohol before she says, "Now say what you came to say." Her boldness and bravery undo me.

"Fuck," I murmur, claiming the bottle and setting it down before I slide off the counter and drag her to me. I swore the conversation came first, but tearing down her stepfather hurts her, and wanting her is just so much easier than hurting her. "You're not alone," I say, because I did leave, I was selfish enough to believe it only sucked for me.

Her reaction is a hard press of her palm to my chest, and an attempted stiff arm I don't allow. I capture her arm, bend it, and hold onto her like I should have two years ago, but she isn't so easily won over. "I can't do this rollercoaster with you, Luke."

"I took the coward's way out," I confess. "Leaving was the cowardly thing to do."

"I don't know what that means."

"I didn't want to see your pain. I didn't want to know I caused it."

"You didn't make Kasey do what he did."

"But as you said at the funeral, pain, and guilt aren't logical emotions. I didn't leave because I didn't want to marry you. I left because it's what I thought you wanted. I left because—"

"You didn't know how to get by the divide?" she challenges. "Isn't that what I said to you last night? You were angry, but we both know it's true. The divide is too big. I know it. You know it."

"No," I say. "No, I do not accept that answer."

"That doesn't make it false."

I cup her face and force her gaze to mine. "I can. You can. We can, Ana." My mouth closes down on hers, my tongue licking against her tongue even as I drag the towel away and fold her close.

She stiffens for a blink of a moment, before she moans one of her sweet little moans, and softens against me, the very act of her submission undoing any further restraint I had in me. I want everything and more, with Ana, right here and now, and there is no turning back. There was never a moment when that was an option. And if it takes a lifetime, she'll know that again.

I rotate her, and lift her, setting her on top of the counter, my gaze raking over her high breasts and perfect pink nipples, even as I press her knees apart. She catches my arms, her gaze searching my face, looking for answers I want her to find. "You didn't come for me until you had no choice."

"Because I knew that the minute I saw you again, I'd be selfish and try to force myself back into your life. Because that's where I want to be, Ana."

"How do I know that?"

"You know me like no one else knows me. You *know*."

Her gaze lowers, seconds ticking by before her eyes find mine. "Blood." She lifts my hand from her knee. "You still have blood all over you." She pushes against my chest, pushes me away in what feels more than physical. "You need to shower. Undress."

It might seem like a fair demand, considering it's Darius's blood, but Ana is Kurt's stepdaughter, and is simply not that delicate, not when it comes to battle wounds and betrayals. Which leads me to believe it's not Darius's blood she wants me to wash off. It's Kasey's and if that's what this is about, I'll never wash away the past or the damage it left behind.

She reaches for the towel and I bend down with her, our hands colliding, a jolt of energy between us. "I'm still fucking crazy about you, you know that, right?"

"I don't know what I know anymore. Please wash off the blood."

"I will," I say, and while there's much more I'd like to say, I force myself to hold my tongue, to give her what she wants. I release the towel and help her to her feet, aware of her naked, perfect body, even as my eyes remain on her face. "Or maybe I should say, I'll try, Ana." I step back, give her space, and then pull the shirt over my head.

By the time it hits the ground, she's wrapped the towel around her body, but I'm also aware of her eyes on mine. Our attraction was always powerful, our hands always all over each other, but wanting each other doesn't mean we can live together. I don't know how I wake up every day and look into eyes that see only the man who killed her brother. I don't know how I walk away from her again, either.

Maybe I'll just keep her so fucking turned on, she can't think about anything else. It's an idea that sounds pretty damn good right about now. I walk to the shower, turn on the water and then finish undressing, the heaviness of her stare following me. Once I'm under the hot stream of water, I regret not dragging her in here with me.

I've tried giving her space, two years of too much damn space.

Decision made, I turn and intend to exit the shower to hunt her down. I never get the chance.

The shower door opens and Ana joins me. Just that fast, I'm hot and hard, and ready to fuck but this isn't going to be a gentle fuck at all. Proven by her proclamation of "I'm angry with you. So damn angry." She steps into me and pushes me backward, against the wall. I drag her with me, cupping her head, and tangling my fingers in her damp hair.

"Show me," I challenge.

"We already did this. I did. I still feel angry."

"Try again," I order softly. "And if this time isn't enough. Try again."

Her eyes glint as she says, "On my terms."

I don't get the chance to ask those terms. She's already lowering herself to her knees, her hand wrapping around my cock. Some part of me still manages to think, though I don't know how the fuck that's possible. Ana feels out of control. She's taking mine. And doing a damn fine job of it, too.

That's the last thought I have before she's licking me like I'm a damn ice cream cone, sucking me off like she's on life support. She goes all in, gripping me at the base of my shaft, cupping my balls, sucking me deep and hard, sucking some more. My shoulders tense where they rest on the wall, my thighs all but buckle. A low groan rumbles from my throat, my gaze locked on the vision that is my cock in her mouth, her tongue swirling around me, licking, oh yeah, licking the hell out of me.

Up and down, she sucks, up and down.

My hand goes to her head, my eyes shutting with the wet heat of her mouth stroking me. "Deeper," I murmur because I have no willpower with Ana. "Deeper."

I can feel her smile against me as if she's won when I've lost self-control. Because that's what she wants—to feel in control—and I sure as hell can't complain. I pump against her mouth. I'm in a greedy place now, and while I tell myself to stop now, to pull out, she intentionally draws me deeper, sucks me harder. She knows what she's doing. She knows I'm right there on the edge.

That's the thing about Ana. She's a fucking wet dream in real life. The girl next door, who is as dirty and perfect in bed as she is out of it.

I come, I do. I come right there in the shower, in her mouth, and she sucks me dry. I feel guilty as shit a moment later, too, when I've never felt that in the past. I just keep taking from her. I pull her to her feet with every intention of pleasing her—God, how I want to please her—but her hand presses to my chest.

"No," she whispers firmly. "You came here to say something to me. Now we talk."

I pull her to me and turn us both, pressing her against the shower wall, and tilting her face to mine. "I know you want control. I know that's what this is about, but I'm not leaving this shower without making you come."

"Asshole," she whispers.

"I'm not taking control, Ana. You had it from the moment I met you. You still have it. Because I have craved you on my tongue every moment of the past two years. That's how much control you have over me."

CHAPTER FOURTEEN

ANA

Luke is doing what he always does to me, what he did from the moment we met: taking me by storm, backing me into a corner—this time quite literally—and forcing me to see him. This matters because he knows what most don't know. I had a wall the size of Texas up when he met me. No one got past it, except Luke.
He did.
It's that storm called Luke.
And I like it as much as I hate it. Damn him and the way he has me pressed against this wall, his cock hard as a rock between us, pressed against my hip. He is the definition of a dominant, alpha male—arrogant, hardheaded, confident, talented both with and without his clothes on—but there has always been a depth of character beyond that persona. A man who cares about everyone and everything more than he lets most discover.
But he did me.
As for me controlling him, I do so when he allows me to do so. He knows when that's what I need or even when that's what I demand and I mean business. He understands the right and wrong times to play those power games, the right time always being when we're naked. And I like it. I've always liked it. All the men in my world, walking around with their dicks in their hands, telling me how big and powerful they are, weren't either of those things. And if they were, I didn't want to know.

But Luke was different. He dragged me to him that first night, kissed me, and left me weak in the knees and panting for more. Falling in love with him was inevitable. Falling out of love with him was impossible. Resisting him now, while we're both naked and he's touching me, is a mighty feat, that far greater women would fail to achieve. But those women didn't just have him stab them in the heart like he did me, either.

"Say what you came to say," I order, the pain of those words prickling sharply.

"I love you," he dares reply, his hands scooping my backside, my breasts squeezed between us, my nipples puckered and aching. As if he, too, is aware of that fact, his gaze lowers, inspecting my nipples, before his eyes meet mine and he adds, "God, you're beautiful."

"You mean you love my breasts," I accuse because no man who loves a woman leaves her like he did me. No man who loves a woman replies like he did to me downstairs. *We aren't married, Ana.* No. No, we are not married. And he's an asshole with a perfect body and a perfect tongue that he intends to use on me.

But that won't change anything.

We are broken, two people who joined together, only to shatter like glass that dropped to the ground, and splintered into a million pieces. The kind of complete breakage and destruction that ensures you can never be pieced back together.

"Hell yes, I love your breasts," he replies unapologetically. "I love every part of you, baby. That I won't apologize for." His voice lowers, roughens up. "I always have. Always will."

Already he wears me down, stirs a longing in me for what we once were, what we once had together. And why am I aware of his cock at my hip when I'm feeling sentimental and angry at the same time?

"Say what you came to say," I repeat.

"I love you," he repeats. "All the rest is just white noise."

"Stop saying that."

"The only way I'm going to do that is to have something else to do with my mouth."

"You couldn't even talk about the sweeter side of our past. It was just a memory of a restaurant, Luke. You couldn't even comment."

He cups my face and stares down at me. "It wasn't just a restaurant, Ana. The first time we went there, we walked the Cherry Creek sidewalks and you smiled up at me with that glorious fucking smile of yours. And I fell in love. That night, Ana. That's when I knew."

Emotions swirl inside me. "And yet you didn't—"

"Want to talk about it?" he challenges. "No. No, I do not want to talk about the night I fell in love with you. Not now, when it reminds me that I can never have that kind of pure, untouched, untainted perfection with you again. But I forgot something important. We forgot something important. Sometimes when things break, they grow back stronger, Ana."

Tears burn my eyes, and already he's on the verge of tearing down my walls. "No," I say. "We can never go back. You're not wrong."

"Maybe we don't want to, Ana," he says, dragging his hand over my scalp and tilting my head back, my gaze to his. My mouth exposed for his taking. "Like I said. Maybe we're better because we crashed and burned and survived."

"We didn't survive, Luke."

"We're here right now, and baby, you're the only reason the sun rises for me. It's been dark as hell without you. Don't expect me to go away this time without a fight. God, woman," he murmurs, cradling my body to his, "you are my everything. I don't know how to make you see that, but I'll spend the rest of my life trying if you let me."

I want to tell him he already showed me he'll leave, he'll leave again, but when we're close like this, his naked body pressed to my naked body, I want to live in this moment.

The rush of heady emotion between us steals my breath, and before I can recover, his mouth closes down on mine and you might as well say he had me at hello. I moan with the lick of his tongue, with the way he lets me taste his hunger, with the way he kisses me as if I'm his next breath.

I'm lost in him, lost in his mouth as it moves from my lips to my neck, his hand on my breast, fingers teasing my nipple. I moan again, a soft whimper of a sound, that leaves no doubt how much I love his hands on my body.

He presses his cheek to my cheek, his lips at my ear, as he says, "I love those sounds. You have no idea how much I fucking love those sounds."

I squeeze my eyes shut, reveling in the low rumble of his voice, in the tight pinch of his fingers on my nipple. Of his teeth nipping my earlobe. I think I might come just from the feel of him next to me, the touch of his hands. His fingers catch my jaw almost roughly and he drags my gaze to his, his mouth hovering, his breath a warm tease. His lips brush mine, and then his hands are pressing my breasts together before he's suckling my nipple. More of those sounds slide from my lips and I don't even try to hold back.

I have not felt this good since the last time he made me feel this good.

His tongue laves my nipple, and my sex clenches with the anticipation that his tongue will soon slide lower, and lower, to that intimate place that craves his mouth.

But he's not done with my nipples, mercilessly moving from one to the other, licking, nipping, teasing, and I can take no more.

"Luke," I whisper when I can take it no more. "Please."

It's his favorite word. If I say please, he gives me what I want. I remember all too well.

He kisses me, hard and fast, a curve to his lips as he says, "Well, you did say please."

He lowers to one knee, pressing his lips to my belly, kissing me delicately, his eyes on my face. I swallow hard with the tenderness of the moment, with the look in his eyes, the way he lingers there, savoring me.

My teeth scrape my lip and he laves my belly button, his mouth traveling to my hipbone. He nips the sensitive flesh there, soothing it with his tongue.

When I think I can take no more, his mouth travels lower and lower, fingers sliding into the wet, slick heat of my sex, right where I want his mouth. His fingers slide inside me, his thumb rubbing over my clit. My fingers find the wet strands of his hair and I hold on, preparing myself for what comes next.

He licks my clit, and when I gasp, his mouth closes down on my nub, and already he's suckling me, driving me wild. His fingers stroke, pump, my hips rocking with the movement. And his tongue, his incredibly talented tongue, is sandpaper one moment and silk the next, stroking me to the edge, then brilliantly soothing the ache. He licks me, strokes me, teases me, taking me to the edge, and then pulling me back, but my body has found its limit. He suckles me just right, and there's no warning. I'm just there, in that sweet spot, quaking with the most intense orgasm of my life. He takes me all the way there, too—straight to the heart of the moment—before he slows his tongue and fingers, and eases me to a place where I'm done. So done my knees start to buckle.

Luke catches my waist, his powerful arm wrapping around me, holding onto me, preventing my fall. The way I thought he'd hold onto me for the rest of our lives. It's a dirty thought, the wrong kind of dirty, the kind that muddies up clear waters with muck and misery. I shove it aside and do so easily when Luke pushes to his feet, cupping my face and kissing me, the salty-sweet taste of me on his tongue.

It's his way of telling me he owns me, and he does. He always has, but it's a good kind of owning me, the kind he reserves for those times when we're alone and naked. The kind that is all about making me moan, making me cry out his name, making me want him more every second of every day. I stole his control earlier. He'll take it back now. He'll turn me around and fuck me from behind, take me in every way possible, and I'll like it. Because I'm confident enough in me as a woman and him as a man, to know there's a line, and we both draw it. And because the only place I can be anything but in control is with Luke.

The only time I can forget, really forget, things like Darius dying right in front of me, is when Luke presses me to get out of my head and in the moment. So now he'll fuck me and fuck me properly. And I'll forget. Until it's over and I can't forget anymore.

CHAPTER FIFTEEN

ANA

Luke does nothing that I expect. He doesn't turn me around. He doesn't demand control. Instead, he cradles me to him, his big body pressed to every part of me, those blue eyes staring down at me, and the fact that he's touching me, that once again he is here with me, is a blessed relief. He hurt me and as much as I wanted to form an immunity to him, it's clear I failed. He is my addiction, and it's bittersweet and terrifying.

"Luke," I whisper, emotion welling in my chest and belly.

"I like the way you say my name," he murmurs. "I really do." His mouth slants over mine, his tongue stroking deeply. And just that easily, I've forgotten about the power play, the need for control. The need to protect myself. I can't think about what it means for him to leave again. I can't think about the past that might well force that to happen again. I'm lost without him. I thought he was fine without me, but not anymore. I think he's lost without me, too.

I sink into him, moaning with how good he feels, my arms wrapping around him. Our water-slicked bodies press together, mine touching every hard inch of his anywhere I can possibly touch. But when his lips part mine and linger, fear pricks at my mind. He can hurt me again. I don't know if I'll survive him hurting me again.

"I'm still angry with you," I whisper. "I hate that you left."

"I know," he says. "But I'm here now and I have every intention of making you mine again. No matter what that takes." He lifts my leg, pressing inside me with a low groan. "Mine," he whispers.

And I know what he wants me to say in reply. *Mine.* He wants me to call him mine. But I don't know if that is true. I don't know if Luke really is mine or not. Not after all we have been through. Not with the betrayal, we both felt, the pain we both created, in each other. He cups my face and stares down at me. "I'm nothing if not yours, Ana. God, woman. Why can't you see that?" But he doesn't force me to answer that question.

He's already kissing me again, and I kiss him back, testing that promise of him being mine on his lips. Testing his vow that he's here now. And doing so with a desperation I barely recognize as my own. For just a minute or more, we're swimming in the moment, in a kiss that is so much more than a kiss.

But from one moment to the next, we need more, so much more.

Luke responds to that burn between us.

He lifts me, and now he's holding my weight with his powerful body, almost as if he's telling me he's got me this time. Or maybe I'm just emotional and reading into every moment with Luke. An easy thing to do when you're in the most intimate of ways with the man you loved and lost.

His mouth closes down on mine and our bodies sway, slow and sexy, and yet tender. This is not sex. This is lovemaking in the way I have only experienced with Luke. But it's different now, a sense of loss and regret, and even desperation beneath the surface of every kiss, every touch, every connection of our bodies. I don't want it to end, but there is just too much intensity between us to fight the build of pleasure in our bodies.

We tumble into our sweet spots, me first, holding onto him, my sex clenching his cock and dragging him with me. I shudder and moan. He quakes and holds me tighter, low rough, guttural groans sliding from his mouth. We collapse into each other, and as tired as he must be from holding me, he doesn't immediately let me go. I sense there are things he wants to say, but for some reason, he talks himself out of it.

He eases me to my feet and strokes wet hair from my face. "I never managed to wash that blood off, not properly. I think that might require teamwork."

He's not just talking about Darius's blood but rather the blood of our past. But he is, no doubt, brutally aware of the fact that Darius represents yet another painful loss etched in a stone of betrayal I haven't fully even processed at this point.

"Yes," I agree. "I do believe it will."

I help him lather up and wash off, our eyes meeting often, a warm awareness between us, latent in history, some good, some bad. We don't rush through the process, savoring this escape from the rest of the world that can't last forever. Too soon, the water turns cold, and Luke turns it off.

Out of nowhere, it seems, I blurt, "I thought he was my friend."

Luke grabs a towel and wraps it around me. "I know, baby. I know. Come." He catches my hand. "We need to talk about some things."

"So, you didn't come to tell me you love me?"

"I did, but we have to both be alive for those words to matter. We need to destroy our enemies, not each other."

He's not wrong. I just hope with every part of my being that we haven't hurt each other too much to come out of this both alive and together.

CHAPTER SIXTEEN

ANA

I resist this conversation with Luke, which he's insisted upon in a rather ceremoniously intense fashion. "We need to talk" is one of those prelude statements that lead to no place good. A conversation that will divide us more than we are already divided, is unwelcome, even if necessary, considering we are hunted by an unknown enemy.

Unknown but close enough to know my family property. Closer to me than I know. It's a realization that hadn't quite hit me until now.

Nevertheless, it's happening, of this, there is no doubt.

With towels wrapped around us, dampness clinging to our skin, and a mix of tension and newfound love ping-ponging between us, Luke and I exit the bathroom.

"The guys brought you some clothes," he offers, indicating the bag on the bed.

"Oh good. I need to wash my clothes, and we should get dressed." I glance up at him. "In case we're attacked." It's a true statement, one supported by our training—readiness trumps conversation—but the look on his face says he's not buying it.

He knows it's about how naked and vulnerable I feel right now, in every possible way, I see that in his all-too-knowing blue eyes, but he doesn't fight me on the delay, either.

"I'll throw our clothes in the wash." He walks into the bathroom, scoops them all up, and reappears before exiting the room all together.

I stare after him, this nagging, clawing sensation inside me, acid burning in my belly that has nothing to do with Luke right now. He's giving me space, and it's one of those moments where I'm reminded that yes, Luke pushes me, and in all kinds of ways, but he pays attention too, he reads my limits. He doesn't even make me push back. He just seems to know when to allow me a moment to breathe.

Like now.

Of course, maybe he too hesitates to lose all that we were in that shower tonight, in trade for a more combative version of the us we have become. I actually hope there is truth in that assessment, as it means he does love me, he does want to hold onto me. Not that I really doubt that he does, but sometimes, as we've both said at one point or another, since Kasey died, love is not enough.

I grab the bag, focused on one thing. Not being naked emotionally and physically with Luke. I can't fix the emotional part but I can fix the physical part. I dress quickly and hurry into the bathroom to dry my hair. My mind is blank. It's a survival thing, something my stepfather taught me, something I used a little too well sometimes. It's how I survived what happened to Darius tonight. It's how I watched a teenage boy die in my arms one cold night in December when he got in the line of fire of a gang shooting on his bicycle. I find a place to store the poison pill of the moment and deal with it at the right time, in the right place.

We both have to be alive for his words to matter, I remind myself yet again.

He's so right. I want us both to live. I don't want anyone else to die, so whatever it is I resist, whatever the discomfort to me, does not matter.

I walk to the door and step into the room. Luke is sitting on the bed, looking every bit the delicious specimen of a man who always manages to get me wet and wanting by just existing. He's dressed in a T-shirt and sweats, the cotton of the tee stretched to the limit, his muscles bulging beneath.

Damp strands of longish blond hair tease his brow, accenting the chiseled line of his jaw, while his blue eyes are probing as they watch me.

"What do you know that I don't know, Ana?"

I hug myself. "Nothing." And yet, I was in that bathroom, avoiding this conversation, he's thinking. And so am I. "Nothing," I say again, but I'm not sure if I'm trying to convince him or me.

"Ana—"

"I don't know, Luke," I say, pressing my hand to my forehead. "And I don't think I want to know."

He pushes to his feet, this powerful figure that has always made me feel like he was strong as steel, and I am strong without him and stronger with him by my side. And despite the uncertainty between us, I am stronger with him here right now. He steps in front of me, his hands settling on my shoulders. "Your head is where mine's at, too."

"No, my head is not anywhere outside of that shower with you, Luke. Other than that, I'm doing that blackout thing Kurt taught me to do. Because you know it's an easy crutch to use outside combat when you want to avoid something."

"Yes," he agrees solemnly. "Yes, it is, but we both know we can't do that right now. People—"

"Are dead," I say. "I know. I do." I wet my lips. "Very few people would be comfortable standing against us at my father's place."

"Agreed." His expression tightens. "It's almost as if these people know the place as well as you, Kasey, or Kurt. Ana, don't you think the way Kurt handled his will was strange?"

An explosion of emotions overcomes me and I twist out of his arms, giving him my back and placing distance between us. I whirl around to face him. "Do *not* go where you're going right now," I bite out. "Do not. I inherit when I come of age."

"You don't even know if there's anything to inherit. He left Kasey with nothing. What if he left Kasey with enemies and debt to those enemies? I was paying him damn well, baby. It makes no sense that he was desperate enough to hold a gun to the head of a princess, or anyone for that matter. He would have killed her and me that day had I not killed him."

"I know you killed him. Do you have to talk about it that openly?"

"Baby, the only way we get answers is to talk frankly and figure this out."

"That doesn't require you openly talking about killing Kasey."

"You think hiding from it makes us survive this?"

"No. No, I don't think we survive this."

"Really, Ana? All that has happened between us, and that's your position on us?"

"Yes. No. *No*." I swallow against this tight, choking sensation in my throat. "I don't want us to crash and burn. I don't. I know you know that." My teeth worry my bottom lip and despite the badass FBI agent that I'm supposed to be, my eyes burn with unshed tears. "I don't. Just—say what you're thinking please."

"You didn't inherit from Kurt and neither did Kasey. This threat we're dealing with hits close to home. You know you always follow the money."

"You think they were dirty?"

"Do you?"

"Kasey found trouble, but Kurt made tons of money."

"Kurt's final affairs don't add up, Ana." He doesn't give me time to get defensive. "Which brings me to Trevor. At the very least, I wonder if Trevor didn't have something to do with Kurt's death. And Ana, Trevor *was* working with Kasey."

My reaction is an instant shove and push, everything inside me exploding in rejection. "You think Kasey had something to do with Kurt's death? Are you serious right now, Luke? *Really*? He was on a mission. Kasey wasn't a part of that. My brother loved Kurt. He *loved* him."

"Kasey wasn't the man you wanted him to be."

"You think I don't know that?" I snap back.

"You didn't see him hold that gun to an innocent woman's head with every intention of killing her, Ana. He was *not* the man you wanted him to be."

"You just said that. Once was enough."

"There's another option. One I need you to think about and think about hard."

"What would that be?"

"Kurt was in the business of training people capable of being killers—"

"Like *you*?" I challenge, and the words are out before I can pull them back.

His expression turns stony, his voice icy. "And *you*, Ana, but that's not really the point. He could have gotten in bed with the wrong people and couldn't get out."

"With what purpose?"

"It could have been that he was being blackmailed, or that he gambled on something that went south and he needed the money. I'll only do it *once* is how it all starts."

"We both know you know that for a fact." I'm speaking of all the kills he performed for the US government, but I'm being petty, I think immediately after. He hates what he let himself become. I know he does. "Luke, I'm sorry," I add quickly. "Forget I just said that. I'm just—"

"Speaking what's in your mind, baby. At least you finally said it. There was a reason you didn't date the men your stepfather trained."

I move toward him and he holds up a hand. "No. Let's say what needs to be said. Kurt was as human as I am. He made mistakes. We need to know if any of them led us here, right now."

"He was dead before Kasey got into trouble."

"Unless he wasn't. Kasey might have inherited the trouble and even a debt that forced him on the path he was on. He hated me. You're an FBI agent. Who was he going to go to? You need to know that I asked Blake to do a deep dive into Kurt's life and death. If there's anything there to find, he'll find it. And I'm asking you to put on your FBI hat and think hard about observations you may have made. Because even if we kill everyone who shows up at your property five days from now, we only kill the body of the best, not the brains." He turns and walks toward the door, and my heart crashes and burns right inside my chest.

"Where are you going?"

He pauses with his hand on the knob, but he doesn't turn. "You need time to think, Ana. About a lot of things."

LUKE'S TOUCH

With that, he opens the door and leaves. When he shuts it solidly behind him, I feel as if we lost every step forward we've taken. I also realize that when we were in the shower earlier, I was reeling over him telling me we aren't married, feeling slapped and shamed. When he told me he loved me, I didn't say it back. And I do, more than life itself. I'm just not sure if he even cares, not after the horrible things I said to him.

Could I screw this up any more?

CHAPTER SEVENTEEN

LUKE

I head down the stairs with every intention of figuring out who I need to kill right now. After all, as Ana said, in not so direct terms—I'm a killer.

We both know you know how that goes.

She was talking about my first kill morphing into a hell of a lot more—too many, the kind of numbers that only a few men in Walker even understand. Savage does. He was another version of me, an assassin for the government. Before Savage, I told myself I was different than the rest of the lot Kurt trained. I was a pilot, and being a pilot drew a line in the sand between me and all the rest. But then, Savage is a surgeon, and a skilled one at that, and yet he only defines himself as a killer.

We don't. He saves lives as well as he takes them.

His wife sees him as a hero.

Though he didn't kill her brother, either.

I step into the living room to find Adam sitting on the couch, watching TV and pigging out of a bag of potato chips. For just a moment, I think back to how I got here, counting on him and the Walker team when I was hell-bent on never trusting a damn soul again after Kasey and Trevor turned on me. Not that I ever really trusted those assholes, but Kasey was family, whether he liked it or not. To my family, my mom and dad, family had mattered. Family was the good, the bad, and the ugly, just as it was supposed to be with Ana and her people.

When I left her, I abandoned my overseas missions for private hire work for the government, doing what I decided back then I did best—killing people, bad people. The job had taken me to Kansas City, Missouri of all places. A small, friendly city, where a really bad guy who'd been hired by another really bad guy, decided to hide out at a Hilton hotel with a woman, a government informant he'd kidnapped. She knew things he planned to torture out of her.

Walker had been hired by the woman's family. The government had hired me.

The hired bad guy was supposed to be alone. He was not. Adam got to him before me, killed him, grabbed the woman, and was about to take a bullet in the back. I killed his intended shooter and then held a gun on him.

Adam, cool as a cucumber, meets my stare and says, "You saved me, man. You actually going to kill me now?"

"Let the woman go and we'll talk."

"If I let her go, you may well take her or kill her. I can't let that happen. Her family expects me to bring her home alive."

"I came to kill her attacker and set her free, not kill her. How do I know you came to do the same?"

"Can I call my family?" the woman asks.

Adam arches a brow at me. I pull my phone from my pocket and kneel, sliding it to her. "Use that."

A few minutes later, I exit the building with Adam and the woman, where a car waits for them. Once the woman is inside the vehicle safely, Adam turns to me and says, "Hell of a good shot back there. I'd be dead if not for you, and she would be as well."

He offers me his hand. I ignore it. He smirks and climbs into the vehicle himself.

LUKE'S TOUCH

I didn't expect to see Adam ever again, but the bastard had shown up at my door only three weeks later to recruit me to Walker Security. It was his way of schooling me on how connected and resourceful Walker could be when they wanted. Adam had convinced me there was a better life than the one that paid me for killing.

I hadn't needed a lot of convincing. There was a reason I was fucked up when I met Ana.

Since then, I've found that Adam's low-key, chill attitude about everything, including enemy fire, works for me which is why he's just about the only human being I can tolerate right now.

I walk to the fridge, grab a beer, and join him on the couch. "What's the word on anything?" I ask, popping open the beer and downing a long slug.

He glances over at me. "Nothing new. Savage and Parker are getting some sleep like we should be. Why aren't you with your woman doing just that or whatever else you'd rather be doing with her?"

I give a small snort. "She's not my woman."

He laughs. "Oh, come on, man. "She loves you. You love her. You'd die for her. She's your fucking woman."

I think about what just went down with Ana, and grimace. She might as well have called me Lucifer. Ana was the one person I believed I could tell everything to and never have her throw it in my face or judge me. But then, everything between us has changed. I knew that. It's why I left and stayed away. I knew this shit would exist between us and I knew that couldn't be changed.

"Sometimes love just ain't enough, man. She knows everything about me, and I mean *everything*, and I should never have told her."

"Ah," he says. "I see. So, you had a fight and things were said."

"She went down that rabbit hole, man, and she apologized," I say. "But she went there. And who the fuck am I to blame her? After what happened with Kasey, it was inevitable. It's part of why I left. I knew she'd have to call me a killer in every way possible. I'd make her worse for the wear in every way. I can't be with her if every time she looks at me, she sees her brother's killer. Nothing has changed. The story is still the same." I down a slug of beer. "I can't be with her. I have to settle for saving her life."

CHAPTER EIGHTEEN

ANA

Fifteen minutes after Luke has left me in a rush of adrenaline, emotion, and confusion, I fight the urge to follow him downstairs.

He won't be alone. I can't say what I need to say to him in the middle of a gaggle of Walker men, and I need to get my head on straight anyway. The truth is, my reaction to what he said was neither rational, considering Kurt trained killers for a living, nor professional, considering I'm an FBI agent.

Luke came to me with a difficult topic to present, but he did so focused on saving lives. As Kurt would say, kill or be killed. We are living those words right here, right now. Feeling anxious, I walk to the laundry to change our clothes. All the while I'm finding my calm spot where I can think, and exclude emotion. All of which delivers me to images of Darius dying right in front of me, but Darius is dead because he was dirty. He played. He paid. That is just how the rules work. I need to call my boss and tell him Darius is dead before his body is found. Actually, I'm sure his body has to have been found already. He died in a pretty public place.

I shove aside thoughts of Darius right now. He's dead. I can't change that fact. What I can change is how I think about Kurt and Kasey. It's hard for me to see them anyway but through the eyes of a person who loved them.

I start to pace. It's how I solve my cases. In the process, I replay events at the ranch, think about conversations, and unravel one moment after the next but I struggle to find answers. Somewhere in the middle of it all, I wash Luke's clothes and dry my own. That domestic task is what shakes me to my senses. I think better with Luke. I figure things out better with Luke. I've spent two years wanting the chance to tell him those things.

I hurry toward the stairs, then down them, and just when I reach the bottom, I catch the voices of Adam and Luke talking. The idea of seeing Luke, of telling him I love him, speeds my pace, but just as I'm about to round the corner, Luke's voice grows louder, his words halting me in my steps.

"She went down that rabbit hole, man, and yeah, she apologized but she went there. And who the fuck am I to blame her? After what happened with Kasey, it was inevitable. It's part of why I left. I knew she'd have to call me a killer, in every way possible. I'd make her worse for the wear in every way. I can't be with her if every time she looks at me, she sees her brother's killer. Nothing has changed. The story is still the same." can't be with her. I have to settle for saving her life."

I sink down on the step and hug myself. I did go there and it was a mistake. Another mistake would be confronting him about this with Adam present. Luke is an inherently private person. The fact that he's talking to Adam at all about this tells me that Adam is a good friend, someone he trusts, and therefore, someone I should trust. It also tells me that I did damage tonight to what was already a fragile shell of what we once were.

It takes all I have in me, but I force myself to push to my feet and walk back up the stairs.

CHAPTER NINETEEN

LUKE

I down a gulp of my beer. "After seeing you with her, and her with you, I can tell you that's bullshit. I assume she didn't like what you had to say about Kurt because he was obviously on your mind when you went looking for her."

"Not even slightly." I set my bottle down. "But damn it, Kurt made big money, and neither she nor Kasey properly inherited."

"Define properly."

"Hers is tied up for years. Kasey was left the ranch but had no money to operate the business. Where's Kurt's fortune? And what kind of nasty people was he in bed with? Ana wants to believe this is all about one package on one dreaded day. I don't think it's that simple."

"Which is why you have Blake looking into Kurt."

"Exactly. She's not even trying to see the truth. And there's a truth there, a dirty one. I keep thinking Kasey, for all his shittiness, inherited whatever that dirt was from Kurt. Or maybe he dragged him into it. Whatever the case, I can't end this by cutting off a tail. I have to cut off the head of the beast."

"Agreed. So, what are you thinking?"

"I need a damn computer, which I don't have, to do some digging."

"Blake's doing that for you. And he's the best of the best. We both need to rest. We have five days until we meet up with the tail of the beast at Ana's property. We won't find the head if we are both sleepwalking."

He's right. I know he's right. "I need to take a jog." I run my hand through my hair. "And yes, I know that's not possible. Is there a damn treadmill or something around here?"

"There's a basement bedroom next to an exercise room."

"That's my spot. I'm going to call Blake and then I'll just sleep down there."

"You sure that's what you want to do?"

"Me and Ana are like oil and fire right now and we're either going to burn each other up or drown in the sludge of it all. She needs some space and so do I."

"You had two years of space, Lucifer. Consider that might not be the answer."

"I'll consider when I have some sleep." I push to my feet and head for the gym, trekking a path downstairs.

Once I'm down in the finished basement, I slip in my earbuds, step on the treadmill, and dial Blake. "Tell me you know something," I say when he answers.

"Man, you gotta give me two fucking seconds. I'm working on it and I've got a couple of our guys working on it."

"In other words, you can't find shit."

"I really can't," he says, "not yet, but I will."

I stop the treadmill. "What does that mean?"

"It means someone made Kurt's financial records disappear, and before you say anything, the man trained assassins for the government. I don't see this as unusual."

"But Kasey took that business over."

"And everything to do with that business is wiped out. I can see Kasey's personal accounts. They're sparse."

Which is why he was running side jobs, I think. "What does that mean in terms of answers?"

"The problem we have is that when someone like Kurt is wiped away, someone like me does the job. We aren't going to find those records. I can't even get to his tax returns."

"Ana's supposed to inherit at thirty-six. Jefferson McDonald holds the trust, or that's what the will said."

"Give me a minute or I can call you back."

"I'll wait."

His fingers punch keys and I turn the treadmill back on. I've been running a good five minutes when he says, "There's no trust. They managed the will, but there is no bank account attached. The firm's records indicate an account held by a third party."

I stop running and turn off the machine again. "There's no money."

"There's no money, which obviously makes no sense. He was one of the most sought-after operations in the world, well-known and well-paid for what he did."

Yes, I think, yes, he was, and he never seemed to hurt for money, but I wasn't around a lot the last year he was alive. I was off trying to make the big bucks before I retired. Damn it, I hate how this is going to gut Ana.

She won't care about the money and I have shit tons of money I'll happily make hers, as well, not that she would want anything that's mine. The problem here is that I'm not wrong about Kurt being in some kind of trouble. "Kurt died when he did something unusual and went with a team of guys on a mission himself. I don't suppose you have a contact who can find out why he did that and for who?"

"I'll dig. Do you know who the guys were?"

"It was a government mission. Jake was with him. We know little else. She wasn't even informed of his death until a week later when Jake showed up." Memories of Ana's knees buckling with the news, my damn warrior princess falling apart, gut me all over again. "He didn't want a funeral and he wanted to be cremated. It was months before we were sent his ashes."

"Are you sure that was what he wanted? Or was he cremated to hide something?"

"That's what Ana was told he'd requested in his will. But am I sure? I'm not sure of anything right now. I need to know who was with Kurt the day he died. Because whoever that is knows more about Kurt than even his own daughter." I scrub my jaw and step off the treadmill as something hits me. "Jake kept logs of the jobs he did on some online program he used on his phone. He was meticulous about it."

"I'll dig. Get some sleep. You're going to need it." He disconnects.

I walk into the bedroom and sit down on the edge of the mattress before I lay back, staring at the ceiling. The day those ashes came in, Ana had melted down. Two days later, we'd driven to the great divide, a place fitting for a man who'd sat on top of the world most of his life, and dropped his ashes. I'd held Ana and she'd quaked in my arms. I didn't think she was going to stop crying.

She hurt that day. She still hurts over his loss to this day. If he's not dead, he's behind all of this somehow. He's the reason Ana is on a hit list. I'll find him and I swear to God, I'll kill everyone connected to this to protect Ana. Even him. I'll give him about thirty seconds to explain himself and make me understand, but I will not hesitate. I'd rather Ana hate me for life than see her dead. And that's where this is headed, with her dead. I can feel it in my bones. And the only way

LUKE'S TOUCH

I've ever learned to survive the bad shit is to embrace it.

CHAPTER TWENTY

ANA

I'm pacing in my room again, as angry as I am hurt over what I overheard between Luke and Adam. Angry at myself for not stopping him when he left the room. Angry at myself for not telling him I love him, too, in that shower. I set that whole situation aside as I stewed over Kurt, but Kurt is dead and thankfully, Luke is not and I have yet to say all the things to him I need to say.

And I'm also angry at him for suggesting he has to leave again. He told me he won't do that to me or us. I halt and decide I need to end this back and forth. I can't promise I won't struggle over Kasey, but I'd rather struggle with him than without him. I need to end this back and forth between me and Luke right now. He is in this or he is out. It can't change every time we fight, because right now, we are going to fight. I don't care if Adam comes along for the ride, but when we're done coming to blows, we are done.

This has to end.

Decision made, I rotate and stalk toward the door, hurrying back down the stairs, but when I arrive in the living room, he's gone and Adam is alone. I screech to a halt, curling my fingers in my palms and willing myself down a notch. Not an easy process, especially when some part of me really needs to see Luke right now. Just see him, just know he's still here, he's still alive and well, and ready for whatever comes next. I huff out a breath and press my hands to my face. When I drop my hands, Adam is glancing over his shoulder at me. He pats the couch. "Come talk to me."

"Where is he?"

"Downstairs running on the treadmill. You might want to let him run off that steam before you go to war. You'll have a better chance of winning. Come talk to me." He indicates the beer on the table. "You can finish that off for him."

Luke's a physical person, which is part of why sex with him is always so intense. He's all in or nothing. I want all in, right now, even if it requires a battle, but Adam's watching me, willing me to join him, as if he has something to say. The man is fighting and risking his life for me. I can't deny his request. I could, but it wouldn't be the right thing to do. I know Luke is here. I know he's one level down. He didn't leave. That's enough for now.

Reluctantly, I accept his suggestion and join him, but I ignore the beer, my fingers curling on the cushions of the couch. "I love him." I glance over at Adam. "I don't blame him for what happened to Kasey, but I never got the chance to fully deal with it, either. He *left*. How is it fair that I never got the chance to even be angry with him? Could he not just stay for me and bear the brunt of that anger and pain? Was that too much to ask?" I cut my gaze. "Sorry. Sorry. You don't even know me."

"I know enough. Have you said that to him?"

"No. He always disappears before I can."

His lips quirk. "He's not gone. He's just on the treadmill."

"I overheard. He wants to save me and leave again. I can save myself."

"But do you want to?"

"I don't want him to leave. But I don't want to be an obligation either." I press my hands to my face again and groan with my admission before I look at Adam. "I threw his past in his face. Just a little, but I did it. He trusted me with that information and I know how it affects him. I sort of opened the door and told him to leave, I guess, right?"

"No. You're human, Ana. No matter what, no matter how it happened, he was the one who pulled the trigger of the gun that killed Kasey. Then he went upstairs tonight and suggested even the memories you have of Kurt are lies. You lashed out. It's a human thing to do."

"Human or not, it caused additional damage we can't afford."

"I don't agree. I think silence, and walking on eggshells, are what cause trouble. Don't just start the fight. End the fight."

"That's my intent, but he always leaves."

"He left once."

"I overhead, Adam. He said he was going to leave again."

"Did he? Because that's not really what I heard. He said he has to settle for less than what he wants. In other words, he wants to stay." I open my mouth to argue that point but he holds up a hand and shifts to face me more fully. "My parents, they're gone now, but like Luke's, they were in love and married a very long time. They didn't live a life without struggles. They just refused to allow them to define who they were as people and a couple."

"Struggles are one thing. This is another whole level."

"Is it? My parents lost a child. There was a lot of blame thrown on one side. They got by it."

"Oh. Wow. Yes, that's rough. I've seen that happen. I've been there when the parents found out. Those are some of the worst moments of my job. How old were you?"

"Twenty-two, which will forever be the worst year of my life."

"I'm afraid this year will be mine," I say, and unbidden, tears burn my eyes. "Because if I find out Kurt was dirty, and Luke and I can't work this out, I'll have lost everyone."

"Can I make a suggestion on how you might think of the Kurt situation?"

"Of course. Luke trusts you. I can see that. That holds weight for me."

"Because you trust Luke," he assumes.

"I do trust him."

"Well, suggestion number one: tell him. If you already have, tell him again. Then hit repeat. As for the Kurt situation, you're an FBI agent. And sure, you could think he hid things from you because he didn't want to get in trouble. But maybe, just maybe, he hid them from you to protect you and to look good in your eyes. Maybe he just wanted you to be proud of him."

I consider the wisdom of his words and decide I already know, but I ask anyway, "What did you do before Walker Security? I'm not sure I remember or that I knew at all."

"SEAL."

"Team Six?"

"I was," he confirms. "Why?"

"Because my father told me you can spot a Sixer if you know what to do look for. They're the elite, the most intelligent, and the deadliest, and somehow still human. It's a unique person, an exceptional person, who can be all of those things at once. I don't know how you connected with Luke when he doesn't easily connect with very many people, but I'm glad you did."

"The feeling is mutual, I assure you. And he connected to you, Ana. He's still connected to you, but you're right. He could easily decide to leave. In fact, if I'm being honest with you, right now I believe he'd die for you before he'd stay for you."

His words might as well be a blade carving holes in my heart, but he's not wrong. I know he's not wrong. "I know," I whisper. "You know I know."

"Then what are you going to do about it?"

"Cuff him to my arm like he did me if that's what I have to do."

He chuckles. "Good plan." He lifts his beer. "Better get to it."

I surprise myself and muster a smile. "Thanks, Adam," I say.

He gives me a nod. "Anytime. I'm sure you'll return the advice."

I laugh. "Loudly and dogmatically probably."

"I would expect nothing less."

I push to my feet and prepare for battle. One where no one dies, but there's perhaps a lot of shouting and a lot of getting naked. If I'm lucky. If I handle this right. I'm not sure what right is anymore except for him. He's right. He's all that is right in my world. With nerves in my belly that outshine any I've ever had on a sting or undercover operation, I walk down the stairs. When I reach the basement, the treadmill is empty, and light radiates from an open door. My stomach knots with the realization that he's planning to stay down here in this bedroom tonight.

I ease toward the door and pause in the opening to find Luke sitting on the end of the bed. Actually, he's laying back on the mattress with his feet still on the ground. As if he was just resting for a minute. Seconds tick by and I realize he's asleep. Exhaustion weighs heavily in my limbs and despite my deep desire to talk to him, I know I have to let him sleep.

There's a chair in the corner and I claim it, pulling a blanket over the top of me. When he wakes, at least he'll know I came to find him. He'll know I'm here. I hope desperately, with every part of me, that in the stormy season we're now living in our relationship, this moment is the first step toward a rainbow. And instead of a pot of gold, we can find each other again.

CHAPTER TWENTY-ONE

ANA

Snuggled under my blanket, with only a dim bedside light illuminating the room and him, I watch Luke sleep, not that I can see much of him but his legs, but it doesn't matter. He's a gorgeous, loyal, wonderful man, who in his imperfection becomes perfect in my eyes. The truth is that he presents himself to the world as the solid, confident, steady figure, arrogant even, at times, but those times relate to work.

My mind flashes back to a day at the ranch. Kurt had invited us out to train, always pushing us to stay fresh, skilled, always growing. Luke had invited me into the combat circle inside the gym. Ten men had watched us, and while Luke was bigger, stronger, I held my own. I'd seen the respect in his eyes that day, as if yes, he realized I was Kurt's stepdaughter. He didn't realize before that day I was one of his trainees as well, and that I had, in fact, trained with him all my life.

It was right after that when trouble started, when Kasey cut in and wanted to fight Luke.

"No," I'd said, facing Luke, hands on his chest. "This is not a good idea."

Luke had captured my hand and said, "It has to happen. You know that."

On some level, I had known. Kasey was combative with Luke. He needed to respect him, but Kasey foolishly believed that because of his years of training with Kurt, he'd win this battle. Luke, however, I already knew, didn't just train with Kurt. He trained with several men of Kurt's caliber and that experience, along with his active duty, made him the better fighter.

It took Luke about ten minutes to lay Kasey out. He could have done it in two. He let him save face.

Kurt always said two skilled fighters would be divided by intelligence, maturity, experience, control, and a good gut instinct. He later told me Luke won on every count over Kasey. He told Kasey, too, and that didn't help matters. He and Luke were destined to always bump heads.

Luke was too much like Kurt. Kasey was too different. Luke's gut instinct told him this hit list originates with Kurt. I need to set aside predisposed notions about him and think about what I've missed. *What have I missed?*

I squeeze my eyes shut and I'm back in the past, remembering the last day I saw Kurt. Luke and I were both leaving on jobs. We'd woken up that morning in each other's arms, naked, pressed close. We'd made love, a slow, sensual joining of our bodies, we'd finished with an hour of just talking. *"I don't want you to go,"* I whisper.

He's tender and sweet, stroking my hair from my face. *"I'm going to buy you your ranch and horses."*

"I'd rather you just stop going on these missions. I'm terrified of the day you don't come home."

"I live that every day you go to work," he replies.

"Thank God you're a badass. Thank Kurt, too."

Two hours later at least, I'd been packing for an undercover mission in Tennessee when someone knocked at the door. It had been Kurt, who never came to me. I always went to him. I drift between slumber and that memory, reliving it. *I open the door to find him standing there, muscles bulging from his T-shirt sleeves. "What are you doing here?"*

LUKE'S TOUCH

"I'm leaving on a mission. Since we'll both be gone a while, I thought I'd bring by those pastries you love so much." He indicates the bag in his hand.

I smile and invite him in, but there's a niggle of unease in me. "You're going on a mission?" I ask as we settle at my kitchen table. "I thought you retired from this kind of thing?"

"Really bad guys sometimes need to be dealt with by really bad guys like me."

"You're not a really bad guy."

"Well, what you don't know won't hurt you, honey." He motions to the bag. "Pull out one of those pastries and hand it over."

I fight the sleep overcoming me, feeling as if I need to be back in that moment, but it's too late. I've been too long without sleep, and some part of me accepts that rest is necessary. I don't know how long that darkness consumes me before there's an awareness in me, something that jolts me to a sitting position. The room is still dimly lit by the side table lamp and Luke is sitting up staring at me.

"What are you doing, Ana?"

"I wanted to talk to you, but I didn't want to wake you."

"Talk to me?" he asks. "What did you want to say? Did you want to tell me I'm a monster? Or a killer? Because I already know." He stands up and walks toward the bathroom.

I have two options. Let him go. Or go after him. I go after him. As I told myself when I came back downstairs, this back and forth ends here and now.

CHAPTER TWENTY-TWO

ANA

I find Luke leaning on the bathroom counter, his chin forward, his shoulders bunched. I don't even hesitate. I slide under his arm, between him and the counter, and wrap my arms around him. He doesn't move. He doesn't touch me. He just stares down at me. "What are you doing, Ana?"

"You asked me that about two minutes ago. I love you, too. I should have said that in the shower."

He catches my wrists and holds them between us, and when he touches me there is an ocean of emotion washing over me. "I know you love me, Ana," he says softly, but there is nothing tender in the words.

"But sometimes love isn't enough, right?" I challenge. "I heard what you said to Adam. You aren't leaving me again. You gave me your word."

"And I was wrong to do so. You will never get over what happened."

"Of course, I won't, and neither will you. But we can deal with it together."

"You said you would never—"

"Judge you? I was defensive over Kurt. It was a horrible mistake to bring up your past. This is an extreme situation we've lived together. I can't ever apologize enough for that. It will never happen again. Just like you will never leave again. Right?"

His jaw flexes at the same time his fingers flex on my skin. "You don't know how to be with or without me. What do I do with that?"

"That was me dealing with this *with you*, Luke. That was me finally getting the chance to work through this *with you*. Because you're here. But when you left, I didn't get to be anything but angry and alone. Why didn't you just let me be angry and get it over with?"

"Angry at me for what?"

"Angry in general. You could have been angry with me."

"I was plenty angry. I still am. I can't do this back and forth with you, Ana. I can't. I'm in or out. I don't know how to be in between and what you're telling me is that that is exactly where you are right now."

"No," I say. "No, I am not in between. God, can you *not just talk to me*, work through this with me? I was wrong to even hint at your past. You are the most honorable, honest, loyal man I have ever known. *I love you*. I have been miserable without you. I trust you. I trust that you did what you had to do because I know Kasey was a fuck-up. I am his sister, I was his sister. I just—I *wanted* to save him."

"And I didn't save him," he says flatly. "He would have killed that woman and me, Ana." He releases me, scrubs the scruff on his jaw, curses, and exits the bathroom. My heart drums in my chest and I follow him, pausing in the doorway, when he's already halfway across the room, to call out. "I am so glad you didn't die that day. I thank God every day, Luke."

He stops walking but he doesn't turn. "I don't want to live another day without you. Please don't make me."

Seconds tick by before he rotates to face me. "I can't look into your eyes and see a monster every day of my life. We can't go back."

"There's never been a day in this lifetime that I looked at you like a monster, not even the day I found out Kasey was dead." I press my hands to the side of my face. "Luke. Don't do this." My hands flail to my sides. "I don't know how to fix this. Can you please help me? Can you meet me halfway? Or maybe you can't. Maybe it's you who's done and I'm a fool for not seeing it."

Twisted in knots, I turn away from him and enter the bathroom. My knees are weak, and now it's me grabbing the sink. I can't breathe. I have faced criminals and gruesome scenes and I survived, but right now, I am not surviving at all. I need to pull it together. I need to find my white noise. I push off the sink and reach for the door, intending to shut it, when Luke appears in the doorway.

CHAPTER TWENTY-THREE

ANA

Luke's stare is piercing, his blue eyes flecked with amber, his mood taut, his jawline sharp, his agitation palpable. He's angry with me. I'm angry with him, too, of this there is no question. But he's also standing in this doorway instead of walking out of the bedroom, and with that one little piece of knowledge, I find hope. And hope, I have learned over the years, can be the tool that builds you up to the highest tower in the sky, only to deliver elation or crushing pain.

I suck in a slow whisper of a breath, and I do not dare blink for fear he will vanish like stardust in the winds of a stormy night and if ever there was a stormy night, tonight is that night.

But I do blink and in that short flutter of my lashes, Luke is standing in front of me, pulling me close, his fingers tangling roughly in my hair. The feel of him next to me, his powerful thighs pressed to my thighs, his hands on my body are bittersweet when I do not know if this is a new beginning or the final ending.

"What are you doing to me, woman?" he demands, his voice a raspy, smoky tone, that draws me into his moody, dark spell.

"Not everything I want to," I dare because I'm done talking in circles, and punching at all the wrong things.

His response is a grunt, just a grunt, and already his mouth is closing down on mine, torment, and passion a wicked mix on his tongue. But the torment isn't new. The torment is a part of Luke, the part of himself that drives him to call himself Lucifer, the part that will always hate himself for what he became and how he lived. But I love him more than he hates himself and I kiss him with that message on my lips. There's a message on his lips, one of hunger and demand. One that demands everything, but I fear he will never offer as much to me ever again.

This idea torments me, and I can do nothing but live in the moment.

I embrace our haze of urgency and passion as we tear at each other's clothes. I am desperate to feel him inside me and I shove at his tee, even as he tears mine over my head, leaving my breasts naked and exposed to his hot gaze. In what feels like moments, I'm fully naked, he's fully naked, and I'm pressed against the wall, and oh God yes, his fingers drag along the wet heat of my sex, preparing me, teasing me right where I need him.

"Holy hell," he murmurs, lifting my leg, and then he's burying himself to the deepest part of my body, pleasure sliding over his handsome features.

He is beautiful in these moments, the image of perfect masculine dominance, a warrior who is somehow more human and vulnerable than in any other moment. He thrusts into me, and I gasp, clinging to him, panting out his name. "Luke."

He cups my breast, pinches my nipple in that delicious way he does just right, and sensations wash over me, settling low in my belly. My sex clenches around him, and I arch into his next pump, his next thrust. He catches my other leg, lifts me, and slides deeper, burying his face in my neck. I hold onto him, cling to him, move with him, and we fuck—that is what this is, but there is more to it for us. So much more beneath the surface.

This is raw and honest, real in every way. This is us. I'm not sure anything since we came together again has been before now.

The rub of his body against mine, the build of passion, comes too quickly. My sex clenches around him hard and fast, spasming with a wickedly intense orgasm. Luke follows me over the edge just as hard and fast, quaking, moaning in that rough, masculine way of his, until our bodies are still and he holds me there, fingers flexing on my back.

Seconds tick by and neither of us move or speak, almost as if we're clinging to the intimacy, afraid of what comes next. But Luke can only hold both our weights so long, and we can only suspend time so long. Caving to the inevitable, he rotates us and sets me on the bathroom sink, pulling out of me but now away. He allows me a moment to right myself, providing a towel to do so, and then presses his hands on either side of my hips.

"All in," he murmurs. "Good, bad, ugly. All in. Say it, Ana."

Relief fills me at where this delivers us. "Yes. All in. Good, bad, ugly."

"Don't do that again," he orders roughly.

"Never again," I say, all too aware that he's talking about bringing up his past and that I didn't just hurt him, I hurt him deeply. "Don't leave again," I order. "Don't do *that* again."

"Never," he promises. "I'm sorry you heard me say that to Adam. I was angry. I was—"

"Hurt," I supply, cupping his jaw. "I'm sorry again."

He covers my hands with his. "It's done. You don't need to keep saying that. Subject over and moving on. What you said about how we deal with all of this was true. These are not normal circumstances and we navigate them best together. I hate I left you alone."

His cellphone rings in his pants on the floor. "Damn it," he groans. "Could there be a worse time? You'd better get dressed." He lifts me and helps me off the counter before reaching for his pants.

He answers with, "Yeah, Blake." He listens a moment and punches the speaker button, before he sets his cell on the counter, already reaching for his pants as he says, "Blake has a message for you, Ana. Blake, she's on the line."

"Ana, Jake's daughter, Olivia, left you a message on your voicemail. I'm going to play it for you."

My eyes meet Luke's, surprise and a question shared between us. "I'm listening," I respond, a knot balling in my belly, dread over what I'm about to hear, what I might learn about Kurt, the only man I really knew as a father. I mean, I loved my real dad, but I was so young when he had his accident, almost as young when my mother had her heart attack.

A moment later, Olivia's voice fills the air. *"Ana,"* she murmurs, a raspy note to her voice followed by a sniffle and sob. *"I'm sorry. I'm struggling to hold it together and even think. I should have talked to you when you were at the house but I just wasn't mentally present. Dad told me that the secrets he was forced to keep from you about killed him. He said that nothing is as it seems. I don't know what that means. He wouldn't tell me. He said that was for my own good, just like it was for your own good, but it doesn't seem to me right now that the secrets were good for any of us. I wish there was more I could tell you but there isn't. Just—well, I hope you hear this. Please stay safe."* She disconnects.

A vise closes on my throat and I'm swimming through the darkness of my mind, seeking light, seeking the truth that remains elusive.

"That's it," Blake says. "I'll give you some time to process that unless you have anything for me now?"

"Not yet," I reply. "I do need a minute."

"You got it," Blake confirms, "but sunrise is about an hour away, fifty-four minutes to be exact. I suggest you both start thinking about getting out of that house. The rest of the team is gathering in the kitchen."

He disconnects. I rotate to face Luke fully, and I say what I feel in my own gut now. "Everything really wasn't as it seemed, was it? You were right. This ties back to Kurt, but I refused to believe he was running a side gig with Kasey. That makes no sense to me. None. Zero. There's a bigger picture here." I try to step around him.

He catches my arm, his jaw flexing, his eyes sharp. "Ana?"

"I'm not mad at you. You got real with me and you know I respect that. I just need to think. I need to put real clothes on and do something. Together. *We* need to do something."

"You know the truth is not going to be gentle, right?"

I think of those early morning drills Kurt put me through and I say, "No. No, it's not. Because I'm done with all the games, in every possible way. Whoever killed Jake killed Kurt. I'd bet my life on it. And we're going to make them pay."

CHAPTER TWENTY-FOUR

ANA

What was once bloody is now Tide fresh.

It's always amazed me how easily blood and death can be forgotten, how easily it can become just a part of the day of a member of law enforcement. But as I pull my freshly washed clothes back on, I am not immune to the fact they were recently covered in Darius's blood. Or to the fact that there were things going on around me that I missed.

"How good of an agent am I that I missed what was right beneath my nose?"

Luke laces his boots and stands up. "You were not around Kurt or Kasey on a daily basis, baby. Don't do that to yourself."

"I was with Darius often. There's no excuse for me not figuring out he was dirty. Had I figured out there were problems, Jake might be alive. Kurt might be alive."

Savage pokes his head in the door. "Boogie on down the stairs, you two. We need to dance party it on out of here." He disappears.

Luke's hands settle on my shoulders. "Had I not left, maybe I would have seen the trouble with Darius."

"Don't—"

"Do that to myself?" he challenges. "I won't if you don't. We need to focus on what we can change, not what we can't." He motions to the door. "Let's go down."

I nod and when he starts to turn, I catch his arm and say, "I am better with you than without you, Luke. Don't get killed."

His lips curve. "I'm Lucifer when I need to be, baby. Love me, you love him." He winks and catches my hand, leading me toward the stairs.

A few minutes later, the whole lot of us—me, Luke, Savage, Adam, and Parker—stand around the island with coffee cups in hand, all of us running on next to no sleep but no one complaining.

"Nothing is as it seems," Parker repeats, after hearing about the message Olivia left. "That helps how?"

"Jake was connected to Kurt," Luke says. "This isn't about Kasey. It's about Kurt. That's why Jake got the hell out of Dodge. Whatever got Kurt killed was too hot to handle." He glances at me. "I know you don't want to hear this, but—"

I jump to Kurt's defense. "Kasey could have dragged him into the mix. I can deal with that a whole lot more than I can Kurt being dirty."

"You don't have to be dirty to find trouble," Luke replies. "Look at all of us now."

"We need a next move," Adam says, glancing between me and Luke. "Kurt's records are wiped out, Ana. Blake tells us this is normal for someone with his government connections. We can't dig into his background. Too much time has passed to recover what's been lost. Where does that leave us?"

I have this quick memory of me and Luke standing on the edge of a cliff in the Great Divide to dump his ashes, and it cuts me right to the soul. The idea of all things Kurt being gone, even his ashes, is brutal on every level. I shove aside the emotional thoughts that

LUKE'S TOUCH

Kurt himself would scold me for, and focus on the matter of survival. Live, don't die, Kurt used to say.

My mind is instantly swimming in the memory I'd had just before I fell asleep earlier. I turn to face Luke, tuning out the rest of the group. "Do you remember me telling you he came to see me the day he left for that mission?" I don't wait for his reply. "I asked him why he was going on the mission. I thought he was retired. He said, really bad guys sometimes need to be dealt with by really bad guys like me. I told him that he wasn't a really bad guy. He said, *well, what you don't know won't hurt you, honey*. He was talking about whatever Jake was talking about. He meant something, *a clue* he handed me just in case, but I have *no clue* what that means."

"I told Blake we need to know who was on his final mission with him but don't get your hopes up. Blake's damn good and well connected, but so far, every road to Kurt is a dead-end."

"And the only person who could have told us is dead. Every time I asked, Jake said it was top secret. He would never tell me." A realization hits me. "The only person we know was connected to this for sure is Darius, and Darius was paranoid. He kept insurance, a way to blackmail those who might wish to control him. Somewhere, in one of his secret hiding places, there is something that will lead us to someone in charge, maybe even the man who had Jake killed. I have to go hunting."

Luke tilts his head and lowers his chin. "What does that mean, Ana?"

"Me and Savage watched a couple of dudes work that place over top to bottom," Adam interjects.

"Yep," Savage agrees. "His house will get you nowhere. They were as thorough as I am eating this delicious sugary breakfast." He shoves a mini powdered donut in his mouth and pretty much swallows it whole. He grins and rubs his hands together. "All gone. Nothing left untouched."

"He wouldn't leave his insurance anywhere expected," I say. "I need to go to the office." I glance at my watch. "It's Sunday. I work in a small field office that's closed, not the divisional operation. We don't have to worry about staff coming in and out of the building."

"No," Luke says. "Not no, but *hell no*. They're watching your office. They'll use you for bait or kill you. I'm not letting that happen."

"I can get in and get out and I have an amazing team to help me."

"We weren't so amazing when Darius got his head blown off."

"Luke—"

"No, Ana."

"We don't have time to argue," I say. "We need to go now. The offices might be closed." I turn to the team. "I need backup, but if you don't give it, I'm going anyway."

Luke catches my arm and turns me to face him, his eyes a hot wash of anger, every line of his body tense. "We're talking about Kurt. Let's talk about Kurt."

CHAPTER TWENTY-FIVE

ANA

My defenses prickle at the idea that Luke's not only going to prematurely convict Kurt of wrongdoing, but my fear, that he knows something I don't know, and he's about to share, here, in front of everyone. "What about Kurt, Luke?" I demand.

"That first night I went to dinner with Kurt, he said: *at some point, if my daughter decides you're a keeper, one day, when I'm no longer around, your job will be to protect her.* I told him I'd die for you, at least a half-dozen times in his lifetime. I didn't say anything about standing by and watching you die."

In that moment, I'm as resilient as a UFC fighter who might have gotten taken down, but relief shoots me right back to my feet. "*And I said*, what I'm saying again now. I can protect myself."

"You wanted me to stay, Ana. Now you have me. I'm here and I'm not backing down."

"Go in with me."

"We're the two people they're looking for." His tone is bullish.

Mine is determined. "I have to do this, Luke. You know I do. And *we* have to do anything we can to end this before someone else dies." I catch his hand. "Please."

Savage laughs. "Give it up, man. You won't win. I never do and time is ticking. We'll all fucking go."

"He's right," Adam agrees. "I've seen the Walker women in action. Let's just do this."

"For the record," Parker murmurs, "I think this is a mistake, but I'll ride high by y'all's sides."

Luke grinds his teeth. "The vehicle isn't big enough for us all."

"Blake had another car dropped off for us," Adam replies, tossing Luke the keys.

Luke catches them, a grimace etched on his handsome face, his gaze flicking to me. "What's the plan?"

"Like it or not, Lucifer," Savage says, "I'm the best killer in the room. I'll go in with you."

Luke's lips twist, and I can tell he bites back a remark, as if the norm is for him to claim he's the best, but he doesn't dare, not with me here. Not after what happened to Kasey. So, I do it for him. I claim his crown. "You didn't train with Kurt," I say. "Luke did and Kurt respected the hell out of his skills. Luke might have earned his nickname in a plane, but he kept it with his combat skills." I glance over at Luke. "You might as well walk in with me. There are cameras. If these people are as sophisticated as they seem, they'll see us, they'll come for us. And that's where the best killer number two can come into play."

"Now I'm going to have to show off and kill me some bastards," Savage proclaims. "Then you can apologize for calling me number two."

Adam tunes Savage out and says, "Blake can handle this," snagging his phone from his pocket and punching the auto-dial. "We need to get in and out of the FBI building undetected. What can you do?"

"I can loop the feed, and control the output of the sensors," he says. "When?"

"As soon as we can get there," I say. "We have one problem. A security guard named Jack."

"I'll handle Jack," Adam offers. "What else?"

"That's it," I confirm.

"If we get split up," Adam states. "Meet at the address Blake is going to text us all in the next five minutes."

"Let's rock 'n' roll," Savage says, tossing keys in the air.

"We'll be right there," Luke replies, and without an argument, the team begins to file out.

Parker is the exception, stopping at the edge of the island long enough to say, "Kurt wasn't dirty, Ana. I'd bet my life on it. I just thought you needed to hear that."

Luke's attention rockets to him. "No one said Kurt was dirty, Parker."

Parker gives a shrug and saunters toward the garage area where everyone else disappeared. Luke watches him every step of the way, irritation ticking in his jaw before he turns back to me, catching my hip and walking me to him. "You don't listen worth a shit, woman. Obviously, marriage no longer means, love, honor, and obey."

"I obey," I assure him, "but usually while naked and without an audience. And we're not married."

"Yes, well, we can fix that, if we stay alive long enough."

Warmth fills me with those words. "Sounds like a good enough reason to stay alive, if I ever heard one."

"Yeah, baby, it is." His hand slides under my hair, cupping my neck and dragging my mouth to his, and kissing me hard and fast. I find myself hoping this is the first kiss of a new tomorrow, but there's a gnawing sensation in my belly that says someone else is going to die before this is over. And I don't know if I can stop it from happening.

CHAPTER TWENTY-SIX

LUKE

I've just pulled us out of the Airbnb aka the makeshift safehouse, driveway and onto the highway when Ana asks, "What was that with you and Parker back there?"

I glance in the mirror checking for trouble and then cast her a quick side-eye. "He disagreed on every point and then spewed that bullshit 'Kurt wasn't dirty' thing, as if he was a guy Kurt confided in." I lift my fingers on one side of the steering wheel. "It rubbed me wrong." *Really wrong*, I think, and I'm not sure why. "So, I'm the number one killer, huh?" I tease.

"I'd apologize or defend my comment, but you know very well that was more about who's more skilled and as your ex-fiancée, present," she pauses for consideration, before supplying, "girlfriend, I will vehemently defend your honor. You're the best."

The term "girlfriend" sits as wrong as Parker's pussy routine back at the house. In the past he kept his mouth shut and apparently, I liked him better that way. I shove aside Parker, fairly done with the topic, and reply with, "Actually, Savage is a badass. Be glad he's with us. He's a surgeon. As in an actual, gifted surgeon."

She blinks. "Really? Savage?"

"Really. Skilled enough to be a renowned surgeon had he chosen to be, but apparently shit happened and he ended up here."

"Ah yes. The shit. It so happens." She shifts to lean on the door, her long blonde hair draped over her shoulder, those sparkling green eyes latched onto me.

Her here, by my side again, *really* by my side, and this—us—talking, is about as surreal as it gets. "Let me get this straight," she ponders thoughtfully. "You're a pilot, he's a surgeon, and Adam's a SEAL?"

"And a master of disguise. I know it's hard to believe because Adam's so damn big, but that man can blend in anywhere, in the craziest of ways. Old lady, janitor, food delivery person, you name it."

"Does he take special requests?"

"No, but I do," I tease.

"Yes, you do," she agrees, "but only when the word 'please' is used repeatedly." Her brows furrow with her shift back to the problems at hand. "You'd think these people, whoever they are, would think twice about coming at this group."

"They took down Kurt, the ultimate beast, with droves of loyal, highly trained students and ex-students. They aren't afraid of us."

"Who is that fearless?" she asks, and at the same time we both say, "The government."

"Or someone with government resources," I add. "It does feel as if this could have something to do with Kurt's government for-hire work."

"Someone in the government at least knows about his final mission," she says. "Otherwise they couldn't have cleaned it up. And they sent me his body. Does Walker Security have anyone inside the government that could find out for us? I feel like if we knew about that mission, we'd know everything."

"I'll talk to Blake," I promise, pulling us into the parking lot of the field office, one small office building among five standalone structures, and note the black SUV parked near the door. "Who is that?"

"My boss," Ana says, sitting up straighter. "They must have found Darius's body. I suspect our team will be here soon. Man down means all men on deck. You can't come in with me, but I'll be fine. Just park by the door and do the boyfriend routine if needed. I'll get in, find out what's going on, and get out."

I pull into a spot and she's already popping open her door. I catch her arm. "Remember my gut feelings?"

"Very well. Why?"

"I don't like this."

"That's called intelligence, not gut feelings. I don't either, but we both know I have to do it. You know I can take care of myself."

This side of Ana, the side who stands up to challenge and refuses to fail, is Ana at her best, and one hundred percent the woman I fell in love with. This is also the side of Ana that I find frustrating as fuck. "I know you're skilled, Ana, but we just talked about this. These people are also skilled and likely connected to the government."

"Thankfully you're right here. I'll be quick. I'll be careful. I *will* come back. I promise." She scoots closer and leans in to kiss me. I cup her face, and drag her mouth to mine, drinking in a sweet taste of her. "Fifteen minutes and then I will find a way to come in."

She smiles and says, "My hero," something she used to call me often and I thought I'd never hear again from those beautiful lips of hers.

She shifts, intending to move away, and I capture her arm. "I really like don't like the whole 'girlfriend' thing."

Her eyes soften and she touches my jaw, with her delicate little fingers and says, "I do. To me, it's the first glimpse of the sunshine rising about the stormy horizon. It works until you make an honest woman of me. I'll be right back."

"I'm moving to the next building, away from the door. If anyone shows up, I don't want them asking me questions."

She nods, and this time when she moves, I let her go, but I don't feel good about it. Not even a little. I watch her punch a code into a keypad and enter the building. Once the door is shut behind her, I shift into gear and drive to the next building. It's close, one of those clustered complexes which doesn't seem smart for the FBI, but that's their business. I park with a direct view of the door Ana entered and should exit soon.

Ironically timed, the sun splays a golden glow of fingers toward the rooftops, but all I see is the blood splattered all over Ana. It wasn't hers and I'm going to keep it that way. Another car pulls up and I watch a guy named Steve Murphy get out and walk to the door. Steve's a seasoned FBI agent who isn't acting like one right now. He never looks around, never offers even a cursory glance toward the parking lot. He ignores his surroundings, rushes to the door of the building, and disappears inside.

There's a knock on my window and I glance up to find Adam standing there. I unlock the door and he climbs inside, hauling two Starbucks cups along for the ride.

I arch a brow. "Starbucks?"

"This is your excuse to go check on her if she takes too long. The boyfriend is bringing her coffee."

My teeth grind.

Boyfriend.

Fuck me, I need to marry her already.

"Not a bad idea," I approve, accepting the cup.

"It's a vanilla latte," he says. "Sorry, man. I have no clue what espresso beverage you prefer."

"A hot one that can burn the fuck out of anyone who touches Ana," I reply, "or better yet, I'll just shoot somebody."

Another car pulls up, and a guy I don't know pretty much repeats Murphy's sins, ignores his surroundings, and enters the building. "I guess when they say Sunday is the day of rest, these FBI agents took it to heart. Any idea why they're here?"

"Blake says there's no report of Darius's body being found at all, but his house was shot up, the FBI thinks he was attacked and assumed hiding out. But now he's cut off communications. They're likely looking for him."

"Let's hope that's all it is."

"Another piece of news: Trevor's dead, man. I didn't ask details, I didn't have time, but Blake said he's calling it a solid conclusion."

There was a time when I wouldn't trust anyone's solid conclusions. Then I joined Walker Security, and I was delivered a new perspective. Trevor is dead. So, if he didn't take that package, who did?

CHAPTER TWENTY-SEVEN

ANA

The elevator creaks like an old lady's bones, moaning and groaning as if the FBI can't afford a decent building. I've always felt like a secondhand citizen here, shoved down the elevator shaft, just below the floor where promotions thrive. From the day I walked into the building, I was Kurt's stepdaughter to my boss and everyone here. You'd think that would indicate I have skills and I know how to use them. Instead, it had stirred a competitive urge in those around me, including my boss.

"You get no special treatment because your stepfather trained half of our men," Mike had said to me, and done so in the first five minutes I'd been in the building. Over time, I'd earned everyone's respect, though the relationship I share with Mike retained a pretentious quality at best.

The elevator dings and the doors open. Olivia's warning is once again in my head.

My heart does this thrumming thing in my chest, which I've come to know as nerves when I'm in denial of those nerves. Nothing is as it seems is a broad warning, and one that I must apply to my workplace considering the closest person to a partner I've ever had is now dead, and proven to be dirty.

Mike does as Mike does, which translates to him being difficult, but could he be dirty, too? I just don't know.

I step onto the second floor of the building to the glow of lights already illuminating the offices. Mike is here somewhere. If I'm fast and cautious, the plan is to get in and get out before he even knows I'm here. I cut right and walk down a short hallway before turning left. My office sits directly across from Darius's office and I step into his doorway and freeze as I find Mike on a scavenger hunt inside Darius's desk.

He grumbles incoherently, straightens, scrubs a hand through his salt and pepper beard, and then turns to face me. He's in jeans and a T-shirt, his fifty-something body still fit and athletic, while his decision-making skills equate to a wet noodle mentality. To his credit though, he's cool as a cucumber, a man who rarely registers much of a reaction, unless he believes no one is watching, of course.

His green eyes darken with awareness. "Agent Banks," he greets. "I see you remain safely sheltered from that hitlist, though might I suggest, you not present yourself in obvious places where you might be targeted?"

"That would be my preference, however Darius and I set-up a way to communicate. He missed our check-in. I'm worried. I came to dig around and see if there is anything at all on his desk that tells where to look for him or what the heck is going on."

"He missed his check-in with me, too. I've got a couple of agents coming in to help me track him down."

And there it is. The confirmation that whoever killed Darius took his body. Which tells me they know just how much heat killing a federal agent gets them and they're buying time.

"Okay, then. That's not good news."

"No. No, I do not think it's good news. Sounds like you still don't know what this is about."

"I don't, but obviously, there's a connection to me and Darius."

"You knew there was a hitlist. Do you know who's on it?"

"I don't." It's a lie or mostly a lie, but it's also the survival of the fittest. *Don't sing to those you do not trust*, thank you, Kurt.

"Then how do you know there's a hitlist?" he presses.

"Jake called and told me right before he was murdered." Mike knows Jake from a few training sessions our team did at The Ranch years back.

He arches a brow. "Jake is dead?"

I don't offer more than a simple, "Yes."

"What does he have to do with Darius?"

"I have no idea. It makes no sense. I was hoping you might know."

"It's not my job to know. It's yours." He motions to the desk. "Look around, then come to my office and let's talk about what the hell is going on."

He moves toward me and I step aside, placing space between me and him, and turning to watch him exit. Only he doesn't immediately exit. He pauses in the doorway and turns to face me. "Just to be clear, agent. I know you're not telling me everything there is to tell. We'll be remedying that before you leave the building." He smirks slightly and then turns and walks out of the room.

I dart toward the door, shut it, and do so with zero intention of talking to him before I leave. At the very least, I do not trust Mike's judgment. That's enough to worry me. I sit down at Darius's desk, hunt through his files, take photos, and come up dry, at least at first glance. I stand up, look around, and eye the picture on the wall of him with his late Irish Setter, Ricky. If there was any place he'd keep something special, it would be with Ricky. I walk to the photo, feel around it, and come up dry. As a last shot, I remove it from the wall and open the frame. Bingo. There's something taped on the cardboard. I pull it free and find a fishhook, a laugh falling from my lips.

It's a clue meant for me.

That man and his fishing spots. If I find the right one, I'll find his insurance and my answers. Hope fills me that answers might be nearby. I replace the frame's setting and hang it on the wall. Now it's time to get the hell out of here. I crack open the door, find my path clear, and quickly head down the hallway. Seconds later, I am rounding the corner, but stop dead in my tracks when I find Agent Murphy and my boss huddled up in conversation at the elevator.

I flatten on the wall, and hear, "She's here?" Murphy asks urgently. "What are you going to do?"

Mike's reply is not a good one. "It's being handled," he states.

Now, all of this could be innocent, but I have to assume it's anything but. I slip back down the hallway toward the emergency stairwell, and by the time I've gently shut the door, I'm texting Luke. *I'm coming down the stairs. Meet me at the doorway.* I don't wait for his reply.

I run downward and when I'm at the door, I reach under my pants, pull my weapon and turn the knob. When the door is open, the coast is clear, but I don't know for how long. I jog toward the main walkway, look left and right, and then left again toward the exit. Agent Ryker, who is a few months new to our team, a transfer from New York, is just entering the doorway, and immediately turns to talk to someone. Ryker is thirty-something, cocky, nosy, and a womanizer. He insulted me one moment and asked me out the next. If I'm sizing up the crowd here today, he is not one of the good guys.

I slide my gun into the back of my pants, where it's readily accessible, but easily hidden, as whoever Ryker is chatting with joins him. That's when I realize that person is Luke, and he's holding two coffees. "Hi, baby," Luke greets. "Sorry it took so long. The coffee shop messed your coffee order up two times. Ryker was going to walk me to your office."

Some people think flowers and chocolate are romantic. For me, the way he calls me "baby" and stands there beside Ryker, ready to kill him, is about as romantic as it gets in my book.

As for the coffee, I'll laugh about this little ploy to get to me later, but right now, I simply join both men and greedily accept the cup. "I need this like I need my next breath." I sip the cold coffee and greet Ryker.

"I'm surprised to see you here, chill and drinking Starbucks," he says. "I thought you were hiding out."

"I am, but the boss wanted to see me."

His brows dip. "He called you in?"

"He did. Almost as if he wants me dead, right?" I laugh, short and choppy. "I better go get lost before I get dead."

His eyes sharpen and he smirks. "Yes. Get lost before you get dead."

Luke's eyes sharpen and he says, "We'd better go. We have a plane waiting." He opens the door. I walk past Ryker and exit the building with Luke on my heels. His vehicle is right up front again and we both walk toward it. Once we're inside, Luke says nothing. He starts the car, backs us up, and drives. The minute we're out of the driveway, I rotate to realize that Agent Murphy is already in his car and backing up. A moment later, a tall man, wearing a baseball hat backward, skateboards into the center of the driveway and starts doing stunts. *Adam*, I think. Master of Disguise. Thank God for him.

I face forward again and hold on tightly as Luke cuts right and punches the accelerator, a harsh reality crashing into me. We're on the run again, and allies are now enemies. *Nothing* is as it seems.

CHAPTER TWENTY-EIGHT

LUKE

I drive in circles though neighborhoods and on major highways until I know we're clear of trouble.

That turns out to be ten miles later when I cut the car into a busy McDonald's parking lot at almost eight in the morning. "Tell me what happened back there," I say.

"Aside from being fairly certain everyone in that building today was dirty, including my boss?" Ana says. "I found this." She snakes something from her pocket and holds up what appears to be a fishhook.

"What the hell is that?"

"That insurance I told you he keeps," she says. "Darius is telling me where to find it. I know he's telling me because I'm about the only person who would understand what this means."

"He had a hook up his ass, dragging him to hell?"

"He liked to fish, though he was horrible at it. He'd go on detox trips, the detox being from his job."

"Where?"

"He had three spots, so I can't be sure which one he's indicating. The idea of insurance is not to make it easy to find for anyone but him. Just that it's possible for me if I'm using my brain. There's his hunting lodge, which is basically a broken-down deserted cabin he stumbled on during some manhunt years back. It's up in the mountains near the Wyoming border. Then there is Cherry Creek Reservoir and Clear Creek Canyon, which aren't that far apart but nowhere near the cabin.

We can't split up, either. I'm the only one who will know what to look for when I see it."

"What's the most likely spot?"

"The cabin. It's the only place he went that didn't have a real lodge. It was just his lonesome spot, but it's also a couple of hours away. The other two are closer. We should go to them first, just to get them out of the way."

"It's a plan. The rest of our team needs to watch your boss and his disciples." I call Blake, let him know the plan, arrange a vehicle change to an SUV for the mountain drive, and then set my Google Maps for a Best Buy. "I need a damn computer," I explain, showing Ana our destination. "Blake and our guys can hack the hell out of a problem, but I'll feel better if I'm doing something to help. We need to find a place to grab supplies before we head up the mountain, too."

"And I need a coat," she says. "But I'll drive so you can hack."

"I'll drive for now," I say and that's what I do. I drive right on up to the McDonald's drive-thru.

Once we're in line, our order placed, Ana glances over at me. "Mike always acted like he resented the attention and respect my stepfather got from the agency. If he's a part of this, whatever it is, Kurt wasn't. Not willingly." She twirls the fishhook almost absent-mindedly. "I'm a common denominator in all of this," she surmises. "I connect the dots between every person involved."

"So does Kurt, Ana."

"Okay true," she agrees, "but the Mike/Kurt dynamic isn't just jealousy. There's something more there." She frowns. "What if it *was* about jealousy? What if Mike wanted to get rid of him, so he set him up in some way?"

"That feels like a stretch, baby. This is bigger than one man's personal feelings."

"While I get that, and I do, what if Mike is involved in something, and he simply thought—*I hate Kurt*—why not use him to solve a problem?"

She's really reaching, but it's not impossible. "We still need to find out what Mike is into."

"I have an idea," she says. "Why not kidnap him, take him to the cabin, and just leave him there until he talks? And of course, I'm not serious. We wouldn't come back from that, but a girl can dream, right?"

This time, her idea isn't all that bad. She can't do it, but if it means saving lives, I'll damn sure do it. But I don't tell her that.

She sighs heavily, frustration and weariness etched in the sound. "Clearly, I'm missing something obvious. As you said, what do I know that I don't know I know? What do we know that we don't know we know, Luke?"

Those are the questions that hang in the air while we eat and as we hit the first two fishing spots with no results. This is exactly why I spend most of those drives on the new MacBook I purchased, looking for answers.

But it's not until I've taken over the driving again, and we're traveling up a winding, narrow road, that I'm reminded of the day we scattered Kurt's ashes over the mountainside. If nothing is as it seems, what if those were not Kurt's ashes at all? It's a crazy thought, one I don't dare share with Ana for fear I'll get her hopes up. I'd thought something similar about Trevor, only to be proven wrong, and for that reason, I mentally try to reel myself back in. And yet, I can't let it go. We're almost to the cabin when snowflakes begin to fall.

"You have got to be kidding me," Ana murmurs. "Isn't it like once in years that it snows in September? I mean, what are the chances of this happening?"

Yes, I think. What are the chances?

It's almost as if the universe is telling me long shots can be real and over and over during the drive, I find myself thinking, what if...

CHAPTER TWENTY-NINE

LUKE

Snow floats in the air around us, gathering in white clusters on the side of the highway.

Ana rests her eyes in the passenger seat next to me, as I had hours before when she was driving. The knowledge that she's my precious cargo has me driving with far more care than I would otherwise, especially during the past two years without her. During that time, I didn't give two shits what happened to me, and I lived every mission with that attitude. I could have, and should have, ended up dead.

The question is, did Kurt end up dead?

This idea that Kurt isn't dead isn't new. I've considered it, especially with his missing money in the inheritance situation, but always in a fleeting and dismissive way. Kurt was protective of Ana. He wouldn't have left her without protection. Hell, if I knew Kurt, and I did, he wouldn't have left me without a word and a warning—protect her, or I've ensured you will die a brutal death.

I glance over at her and smile at the way her hair is now draped over her face. God, I love this woman. This is exactly why I need to tamp down on my urge to talk to her about Kurt possibly being alive. It's a long shot. I don't want her to get her hopes up or question why he would fake his death. Okay, she'd know why he was faking his death. He's running from something. The real question would be why he didn't let her know he was alive.

I rummage through my memories, trying to think of something, anything Kurt might have said to me that would have given me a clue I can decipher. Of course, Kasey was in the picture, and for all I know, he knew what Ana does not, but then again, Kurt didn't respect Kasey much. He loved him, but they weren't blood, and Kasey didn't perform to Kurt's standards. Ana did. Ana was the son he never had. He didn't even need me to fill those shoes. She was both his princess and his warrior.

He can't be alive. He would never leave her in the dark like this. I'm about to fully dismiss the idea of his faked death when I have another jarring thought. Kurt was a powerful man. If he felt the need to fake his death, the heat was hellish, and the problem was massive. And along those lines, if he didn't tell Ana, he had a good reason. She would have gone after the problem, attacked like a lion, who would never have allowed its prey to survive. As much as he trusted me to protect her, he knew what I know, too. I would have had to lock her away in a cave somewhere to keep her out of trouble.

She's an FBI agent and she takes that seriously. FBI agents don't look away. Family does not look away. Damn it to hell, but I did when I left.

Ana stirs beside me, stretches, and sits up. "How is it snowing this much?"

"It's Colorado, baby. It likes to do wild and crazy."

"That it does," she agrees. "How close are we?"

"Based on the directions you gave me, about an hour out."

"Well, let's hope I'm right because I only came out here with him one time."

"Yeah, about that," I say. "Tell me again why you came to a secluded place with Darius?"

She laughs. "I know you do not think I fell into Darius's bed when we broke up."

"I know he would have, he liked you, too."

"You also know I told you I didn't fall into anyone's bed and I don't want to think about you doing so."

"Baby, you are it for me. Anything I did was me trying to survive you hating me."

"I could never hate you, Luke. Pain is just a brutal emotion."

No words have ever been truer, which drives home why I can't tell her what I'm theorizing about Kurt until I know more than I do now. Unfortunately, up here in the mountains, I may not even be able to share those theories with Blake.

The snow falls harder now, and I focus on the road. "Check your phone, baby. Do we have service?"

"I already did. And we do not."

I glance behind me in the mirror, ensuring no one is following us. The only way being cut off from the rest of the world while being hunted by a dangerous enemy is really being cut off from the rest of the world, is if we're *really* cut off from the rest of the world.

CHAPTER THIRTY

LUKE

The cabin is an absolute shithole, and with the snow suffocating us in every direction, it's our only form of shelter in sight. I park the SUV behind the broken-down wooden structure, out of the line of sight of anyone approaching. Once me and Ana have pulled on our coats and covered up with our hoods, I say, "Let's do this, baby."

We exit into the cold, snowy, early evening, not much sunlight left to pierce the clouds and allow us any opportunity to search. The temps are chilly but not freezing, however with the snow coming down this hard, it's going to build up. It's already building up. Thank fuck my inner survivalist urged me to buy supplies and we're prepared for this, but I'll come back for it all after I know what's inside. For now, I grab a lantern, and leave the rest. Hurrying toward the cabin, we climb the surprisingly solid steps, and find a lock on the door with a key code.

"Let's hope it's the same as it used to be," Ana says, punching in a code, and bingo, we're in, with the bonus of expecting no one else to be waiting inside, but I never assume anything when it comes to Ana's safety.

I motion for her to hang back, crank up the lantern, and open the door, the scent of dust tormenting my nostrils, but it's far better than the stench of death we might have found. I'm prepared for anything with the shit we have going on. For now, I'm greeted by nothing but a worn-out ancient brown couch, a couple of equally worn chairs, and a stack of firewood. Darius made this place his own all right. It's not that cold out, forties maybe, twenties later tonight up this high. In this environment without a fire, we'd be chilly as fuck.

"I'm going to grab the other lantern," Ana calls out as I make my way to bathroom and what I assume to be a bedroom.

I wonder whose land we're on, and kick myself for not checking that before we came up here. What drew Darius to this location? What was the case? Who was it connected to and why? All questions to ask Ana and find out.

I check the one back bedroom, and then call out to Ana. "All clear."

She doesn't answer.

"Ana?!"

When she doesn't answer this time, it's a gut punch, and I'm moving forward, setting the lamp on a wooden table and rushing toward the door. I step onto the porch and Ana is nowhere to be found. I fight the urge to call out to her again, drawing my weapon, with the fear, that I was wrong. We are not up here alone.

I'm moving toward the truck, scanning the area as I do, my gaze cutting through the snow, with no movement to be found. Damn it to hell, the cool, calm soldier that I am is not cool and calm right now. I round the cabin and bring the truck into view, finding my way to the passenger side where Ana's bag is sitting on the ground. Footsteps are scattered about the snow, leading toward the woods directly behind me and I swear a part of me dies right here and now at the idea of her being dead. Gone. Lost forever. Why the fuck did I take my eyes off of her?

Already, I'm racing toward the woods directly behind me, promising myself I will get her back. Telling myself she has skills, more than most anyone I've ever known. She will survive. She is going to be okay. I run left and right and all around, following random footprints, that all look like Ana's. None of them are larger. This realization comforts me but why would she come out here.

I walk the area fast and thoroughly and find nothing. Holy fuck, I cannot lose Ana. I snag my phone, check for service and come up with no bars. I can't call her. I start running back toward the SUV, praying Ana will be there, reaching for the moment I clear the trees again. My relief at bringing the vehicle into view is momentary when she is not there, obviously, my hopes were hung on the false hope that she'd be there looking for me.

I round the front of the truck and find footprints leading to another area of the woods, toward the front of the cabin. I run that direction and bypass the woods. Once I'm at the front door of the cabin again, I step inside. "Ana?!"

There is no reply.

Ana is not here.

CHAPTER THIRTY-ONE

LUKE

"Luke."

At the sound of Ana's voice, I turn to find her walking up the steps, her weapon in her hand. My relief is as mighty as a hurricane and I meet her halfway, catch her to me and kiss her hard and fast. "What the hell is going on?"

"I heard something," she says, stepping inside and shutting the door. "I know I heard something, but more so, I felt like I was being watched, but I can't find footprints. I can't find proof that anyone is here."

"How about telling me, woman? You took off and I couldn't find you. Do you know what was going on in my head?"

"Sorry, but—"

"Sorry doesn't cut it, Ana. I thought you'd been kidnapped or worse, you were dead."

"Yell at me later. I felt like I was being watched, Luke."

"As you said, there are no footprints that aren't yours."

"Right. I know. I'm sure it was an animal, but I'm uneasy now. I want to search the cabin and get out of here."

"We aren't going down those narrow roads with a drop-off mountain in this weather. We're safer here. Stay here. Search. I'm going to go get our supplies and start a fire."

"A fire will make smoke. That's just going to announce our presence."

"If anyone that matters is here, they followed us and the smoke won't change anything. Otherwise, it won't make a difference." I start to move away and Ana catches my arm.

"Luke—"

"Baby, I trust your gut instincts. You know I do, but we're here. If there's a battle to fight, this is where it's happening and I wouldn't count us out. We're pretty badass, especially together."

"Yes," she says. "Agreed. But I'd like to live to enjoy that."

"You will. We will." I kiss her. "I'll be right back."

"Maybe I should cover you."

"Do the search in case things get too hot to do it later."

She nods and by the time I'm at the door, her gun is on the wooden kitchen table, and she's squatted down, checking the underside of the wood. Damn, this woman is going to be the death of me, but she's also my life. I'm not going to let anyone take her from me.

I exit to the porch and shut Ana inside the cabin, and for long moments, my gaze scans the area, seeking out any sign of life. My eyes find no evidence, but Ana's right. There's a distinct presence.

"Is that you, Kurt?" I whisper because my gut says we're safe right now. And perhaps because I want my theory to be correct. I took Ana's brother from her. It would be a hell of a gift to give her back Kurt.

A few minutes later, I walk back into the cabin loaded down with bags. "It's snowing like crazy out there."

"Anything other than the snow out there?" Ana asks.

"A deer and a couple of bunnies," I tell her, leaving out my shared sense of being watched. Or rather, of someone being here. Being here does not mean whoever this is means to hurt us. Darius hung out up here. Maybe someone else does as well."

"Maybe it was a deer I felt watching me."

"More likely a bobcat or a cougar, a predator that was sizing you up for dinner and didn't know I've already claimed you as mine."

Her lips curve. "Leave it to you to turn this into sex."

"What's wrong with turning this into sex?"

She laughs her delicate little laugh, that defies how tough as nails she is. "Nothing."

"Well, then I better start a fire because I know you. If you're cold, I'm not getting your clothes off of you."

"That is true," she agrees. "While you'll take your clothes off quite easily."

She's talking about us, I know this, but I regret telling her that I bedhopped while we were broken up. Not that it was like I cheated. I thought she was done with me. But I don't know that she needed to know. Seems I just keep finding the sludge to muck about in.

"Only if you say please, baby," I tease, grabbing some fire starters out of the bag I set on the chunk of wood, and not much more, being used as a coffee table. "Any luck finding that insurance?"

"None," she says, "but I know it's here somewhere."

I believe her. The fishhook, the cabin that's been prepped. This was Darius's place. Whatever there is to find, it's here somewhere. "I'll help you look when I'm done here." I throw the last log I need on the fire, and light a fire starter, using it to stoke the flames in several places.

Once the flames have cranked to a healthy glow, Ana joins me, warming her hands and smiling up at me. "You're right. I hate to be cold." She glances at the couch. "But that couch is so dusty that we might get dust in all the wrong places without our clothes on."

"Good thing I bought a blanket."

Her smile widens. "You think of everything, don't you?"

"When it comes to getting you naked, I do." I give the fire one last once over and pull her close. "Before we test that blanket, let's find what we came for. Where have you looked?"

"The kitchen. That's about it. I did find some bottled water in the fridge and a bottle of some sort of scotch."

"Darius knew the basic necessities of life, clearly."

Her smile fades. "He was dirty. Apparently, the basics weren't enough."

"Maybe there was more to the story, Ana. Maybe that's what you'll figure out when we find his insurance." I kiss her forehead. "Everything is not what it seems, remember?"

"He wasn't what he seemed," she replies. "I'd say that fact resembles that statement completely." Her brows dip. "There's a deer stand he turned into a little fishing spot by the water. Let's go down there before it gets too dark."

"It's all but there now."

"We have flashlights," she says, already sliding into her coat. "That's the place. I know it. That's where we get our answers."

I want answers as badly as she does, therefore, against my better judgment, I'm easily convinced. I grab my coat as well and slide it into place. The bottom line is that if someone is out there, they will be out there later as well. If that someone attacks and we have to run, we want to run with Darius's insurance in hand.

LUKE'S TOUCH

With flashlights in hand and our weapons on our persons, easily accessible, I open the door, and we leave the shelter of the cabin.

CHAPTER THIRTY-TWO

LUKE

The snow pummels us to the point that had the ground been cold, we'd be in six inches right now instead of one. A good thing, considering we literally hike a solid mile to arrive at our destination. Considering we're also at a high altitude and the temperature is dropping fast, while the snow shows no signs of slowing down, we need to find what we're looking for and get back to the cabin. The lake comes into view, Ana points right, and we begin another half-mile walk.

"There it is," Ana says, tugging my coat and pointing to a deer stand inside a cluster of trees that's obviously been moved here with the purpose of fishing. Deer don't exactly walk on water or swim.

With the sun rapidly crashing, our flashlights guide our path forward, and once we're at the shelter, Ana squats down in front of it. "You coming?"

"Who doesn't want to crawl in a deer stand in the middle of snow? Of course, I'm coming in."

She laughs, shines her flashlight into the structure, and then crawls inside. I quickly follow, icy cold snow on my palms, the wind at my back. The space is big enough for three, and Ana and I prop our flashlights up and brush off the snow.

"Now I'm cold and ready for that fire," she says, looking around at her surroundings and pointing up, toward some sort of tarp covering the steel roof, which seems to serve the purpose of keeping us dry. It would also make a good hiding spot and I reach to the right where it's anchored on a nail and pull it down.

Something falls down on top of us and Ana reaches for what proves to be an insulated bag. "Jackpot," she murmurs, as I reattach the tarp to block the snow.

Ana eagerly unzips the bag, and I aim the flashlight at the contents. There's a notebook and a gun inside a plastic bag, and a tape recorder.

"You weren't kidding when you said he keeps insurance."

"A gun," she says. "This feels dirty in every possible meaning of the word."

"Did you expect anything less?"

"Maybe it's not what it seems and Darius was actually one of the good guys. He did leave this for me to find."

"I won't be convinced that's a gift instead of another problem until we inspect the contents." I ease forward and glance outside, checking the worsening weather. "And as eager as I know you are, we can't do that here, now. It's too early in the season and it's been too warm during the day for me to feel like this storm is going to actually bury us, but we can't take any chances out here. We need to get back to the cabin before we get buried out here."

Ana rezips the bag and since I want her hand free should we run into trouble, I grab it before exiting the shelter. Once I'm on my feet, I pull her to hers. Soon, we're going to find out what Darius knew that we don't know, and I fear some of it might come as a blow Ana does not expect. If that proves true, we'll deal with it, as she herself said: better together than apart.

We start the hike back to the cabin, our footsteps already covered by snow, which means no one can track us, but in turn, we can't see anyone who might be tracking us. Thus far, there's been no sign of anyone, and I no longer have the sense of being watched, nor has Ana brought up a further concern. Big cats are stealthy predators who will stalk and kill, with the kind of stealthy skill of a damn superhero. The possibility that we were simply dealing with a wild animal is a real one. Not our enemy and not Kurt.

I haven't allowed myself to consider the idea that Kurt could be the enemy.

Finding him alive under those circumstances would equate to nearly the same pain to Ana as me pulling the trigger and killing Kasey. And that's not a world me or Ana want to live in. It's not one we'd both survive.

CHAPTER THIRTY-THREE

LUKE

Upon our return to the cabin, we finish searching it and drape our coats over the kitchen chairs to dry. The fire burns low and I immediately throw more wood on to burn. Ana unwraps the blankets we purchased at the store and drapes them over the couch, setting bottled water and protein bars out for our evening feast.

When we finally sit down on the couch, the insulated bag sits on the coffee table, between us. "Why am I not ripping it open?" Ana asks. "What am I afraid of? I want this over. In premise, what's inside that bag allows that to happen."

I squeeze her leg. "Maybe a part of you doesn't want to know just how involved in all of this Darius was."

"No," she says. "I want to know everything."

She reaches for the bag and unzips it, folding back the lid. She reaches for the gun in its plastic bag, which is not labeled. "Obviously this has someone's fingerprints on it and a connection to a crime. There's no other reason why it would be bagged and hidden out here."

"We'll have Blake check out the serial number and the prints. He can keep it off law enforcement radar."

She sets the gun down and reaches for the tape recorder. "This is the gold," she says. "I'm certain of it." She draws a breath and hits play. A few moments later, a male voice is speaking to us.

September 5th.
Ana.

Ana murmurs, "It's Darius," her fingers lock together in front of her.

If you're listening to this, I clearly ended up dead and that sucks. I'm pissed about it, oh yeah, I am. I'm sure you're pissed at me, too. I'm sure you found out some things about me. I wish I could tell you this recording was me explaining how I got blackmailed into bad decisions, or how what I did saved even one life. It's not. Bottom line, I got greedy. I was tired of watching the criminals get rich and the good guys get dead. I figured I might as well get rich and get out.

Ana pauses the recording and looks over at me. "Damn it and damn him."

"He paid the ultimate price, baby. Now, all we can do is try to save the lives he didn't."

She nods and turns the recording back on.

I'm not going to get into the when, why, and how bullshit, Darius continues, *inside the notebook, you'll find a list of packages that I know were delivered, which dates, and buyers names. I don't know what was in the packages. I didn't want to know. I wasn't even involved in that side of things, but you know how I roll. I wanted to know what I as involved with. I did some digging. I followed someone important to the operation. I recorded his conversations. I took photos. There's a key in the bag. It goes to a lock box loaded with that shit.*

On to the topic of Kasey...Yes, let that sink in a moment—on to the topic of Kasey.

Ana's spine stiffens a moment and then she leans forward and rests her chin on her hands in obvious anticipation. My hand goes to her back, flattening there, silently letting her know I'm right here, I'm not going anywhere, ever again. The recording continues.

You'll find the one Kasey was delivering highlighted. The buyer won't know who the big boss was, because there was a front man. That would be our boss, Ana. Mike is the one who pulled me into this. He laughs. *See, I said I wasn't going to talk about the when, where, and how or any of that bullshit, but turns out I have to in order to get you this information.*

I repeat, Mike is the front man. I've given you plenty enough to put him away for life, but he'll end up dead before he sees a week in jail. These people are powerful. Don't move on this until you have the head of the beast. Don't move on this personally, either. Keep your name out of it. They're international. Take these fuckers down in another damn country. Get Luke involved, Ana. That bastard has skills and they just multiply. He laughs again. *Yes, that's a play on an old eighties tune, you know how I loved the eighties. And Luke loved you, and Kasey...well, Kasey wasn't a good guy. I know you know that, but I also know love is blind and shit. He was your brother.*

Something to keep in mind.

That list of buyers includes some of the richest people in the world. They'll have money and resources to kill any effort to destroy this operation. But if you get the right ones behind closed doors, maybe they'll help you rather than hurt you, just to save themselves a hell of a lot of trouble from law enforcement.

Last but not least, I made a wad of cash, because they wanted you and your family monitored and to keep your nose out of Kasey's business during delivery windows. It seemed like easy cash. Kasey was going to do what Kasey was going to do anyway. Yes, I was betraying you, but I thought Kurt could handle himself and Kasey, so it was all good. Mike hates Kurt, by the way. It runs deep. There is something there between those two, something deeply personal.

No, I don't know what.

Anyway, my paycheck got bigger after Kasey died and that package disappeared. Trevor never had it, but they killed him so he couldn't talk. He had loose lips and you know how loose lips get you dead. Actually, they say loose lips sink ships, but they aren't us, now are they? For reasons I don't understand after Kasey died, and the package disappeared, they doubled my pay to report on your activities. At one point, they thought you had the package but I convinced them that if you did, you didn't even know you had it. I tried to get them to tell me what it was so I could look for it and get the heat off of you. They wouldn't tell me.

Something happened last week, though. Mike took a phone call. I managed to get pieces of it. Someone was trying to sell whatever was in the package. It had resurfaced. They didn't know who, but the big boss felt like a fool. He looked bad to his client. He was pissed. People had to die. I guess I was one of those people.

Okay, that about sums it all up.

I suck. I did you wrong. I get that. Maybe you should have dated me and kept me in line. I'm not kidding, but you know, it is what it is. We didn't happen. But I do have one last parting gift. You'll figure out what it is. Keep looking. Hasta la vista, baby. Okay, probably not. I'm pretty sure I'm in hell. You better not show up here.

The recording ends.

Ana doesn't look at me. She digs through the box and finds an envelope with her name on it, lifting the flap to pull out a card. She reads it and hands it to me, pressing her hands to her face. The card reads: *Ten million dollars in cash. It's buried at the coordinates below. You could always just walk away, Ana. And that's what you should do.*

Holy fuck.

"Ana," I say.

She pops to her feet and turns to face me. I'm standing with her when she says, "We have to go back. We need to—"

My hands come down on her shoulders. "Wait out the storm, go through all the information, and then get on a secure phone call with Blake."

"I need to do something, anything. I need to fix this. We need to go get that bastard Mike talking. I need to know how Kurt was involved and I need—"

I cup her head and kiss her, molding her close, holding onto her a little too hard, but I don't care. She needs to be held right now.

CHAPTER THIRTY-FOUR

LUKE

I slant my mouth over Ana's, deepening the kiss, the sweet honey taste of her on my tongue along with a hell of a lot of resistance. She's stiff, fighting me, because she really wants to fight a battle she cannot win, not now, not in the mountains in the middle of a snowstorm. Maybe not ever, not if the secrets revealed destroy all she knew of the only father she really ever knew. My hands travel up and down her back and she moans.

"Luke," she pants out. "We can't do this right now."

But she doesn't push me away. Her fingers twisting around the cotton of my T-shirt, her body softening against me.

"We can't do anything else *but this* right now," I assure her, my fingers curling around her neck to lift her gaze to mine. "Let it go for now."

"I want to, but—"

My lips brush her lips. "*Let it go, baby.* And you owe me. You said if I started a fire, you'd let me get you naked. Remember?" I catch the hem of her shirt.

"What if Kurt was involved, Luke?"

I drag her shirt over her head and toss it aside. "There's nothing you can do to change anything he did or did not do." I run my hands around her back and unhook her bra, and when I would drag it away, she catches it to her.

"What if someone was watching us earlier?"

"If I die naked and inside you, Ana, I'll die a happy man."

She laughs, a distinct shift in her mood, a hint of the intensity sliding away. "You're crazy."

"For you, baby," I assure her, easing her hands down and dragging her bra away, my mouth trailing her jawline, her neck, her nipple.

Her fingers dive into my hair. "You're not listening to me."

I am listening, I think. Which is exactly why I'm forcing her to be here, to be present in the moment and thinking about me, not Darius, not Kurt, not Mike or any of those fools. But I don't say that. Instead, I kiss her again, smiling against her lips. "Your naked breast is in my hand, baby. I'm only capable of so many words." I thumb her nipple.

"Hmmm," she murmurs.

It's the sound of submission, of her letting go of everything but me, and us, this moment.

If I wasn't already hot and hard, that sound would get me there.

It's also me submitting to the absolute control she has over me, even in those moments when she thinks she does not.

I turn her with me and sit on the couch, my hands gripping her hips. My lips press to her soft skin, tongue laving her belly button. Her hands are back in my hair, finger curling around random stands, the tug of her grip all about encouragement and her need for my mouth to move lower.

My gaze lifts while hers lowers, the heat between us seared by emotion, and I can feel the rise of possessiveness in me. No one will hurt her. No one will ever hurt her again. Not with me in the picture. I will kill for her. I will cause pain for her. And I will tell the world, and even the devil himself, to back the fuck off.

I reach for her zipper. She catches my hand. "Together."

There were times in the past, many in fact, when Ana and I played games, where I demand control, and she wants to relax into the comfort of not having to be in control. But Ana always knew in those times that she was ultimately in control, that she chose to use those games to allow herself a break from everything around her. But a break isn't what she needs right now. Control is what she needs, which is exactly why she wanted to run out of the cabin and charge through the snow to return to the city. Right now, if I push her, she'll suffocate.

Right now is about us on the most intimate of levels.

I push to my feet and we undress together. There is a familiar comfort in the two of us, a bond that has never faded. I can feel the threads of our two separate lives melding together, unbreakable, when we once were not. That strength will be how we survive, not just what is ahead of us, but all the bullshit that all but destroyed us. I catch Ana to me and sit down, dragging her onto my lap. Her hands settle on my arms, her naked breasts between us, my erection pressed to her belly.

My fingers slide under her hair to her neck and I drag her mouth to mine. "Better together, right, baby?"

"Yes," she whispers. "Better together."

"They're going to regret who they messed with," I promise her.

"God, yes, they are," she murmurs as I lift her, shifting us, until I'm pressing inside her, and I groan with the warm, tight heat of her body.

Ana scrapes her teeth across her lower lip, her fingers digging in my shoulders, and it's sexy as fuck. She's sexy as fuck. My body demands a fast and hard path to satisfaction, but I damn sure plan to savor every moment of this. I cup her head, and we breathe together. Ana's hand presses to my cheek and she pulls back to stare down at me. "Is it crazy for me to say I can finally breathe again?"

Holy hell, the things this woman makes me feel. I can't even put a name to the rush of emotions those words deliver. "No," I say. "No, it is not. I feel the same. You're the love of my life, baby. Don't ever forget it."

She smiles at my answer, a sweet smile made sweeter by her passion-laden eyes, and the squeeze of her body around my cock. She leans in and presses my hand to her breast, and her lips to my mouth. Now I'm the one smiling and we laugh for no reason at all. Fuck me, it's sexy as hell. I pinch her nipple and she flattens her hands on my chest, arching against me, silently urging me to stop holding back, to move with her.

I drag her mouth to mine, kiss her, taste her, shifting our hips as I grind her against me, shifting a little left and right. She gasps and moans with the sensations it creates. *Oh yeah, baby*, I think. She arches into me again, rocking her body. At the same time, the licks of our tongues grow wilder, hungrier. I mold her closer, pressing her breasts to my chest, the feel of her next to me, driving me to the edge of insanity. But still, I hold myself back, savoring what becomes a sultry dance between us.

There is a moment though, when she catches a handful of my hair, just a hint of that wilder, darker side of who we can be together, showing itself, as she whispers, "Luke. *Please.*"

That's it. We're done going slow. I lift my hips, thrust, repeat, and she rocks hard and fast against me until she's burying her face in my neck, her body trembling, her sex, clenching my cock. I groan, with the

sensation deep in my balls, and then I'm holding onto her a little harder, shuddering with release. When our bodies still, Ana melts into me.
"Oh my God," she murmurs.
I smile against her neck. "Yes. That." We shift our bodies, and she rushes to the bathroom while I lay pull on my pants. Do I think someone is about to attack us? No. But do I want to be ready in case? Yes. And I damn sure could shoot them naked, with my cock hanging out, but it would be really damn awkward. Ana returns and I slide a blanket around her and lay down, pulling her on top of me. Yes, I'm greedy. I don't want her to get dressed yet. I'm not done with her. If I'm lucky, she's not done with me either.

But there is a topic we brushed off for too long now. In fact, I told her I didn't give two fucks on this topic and at the time I didn't. But things have changed. We've changed. "Are you on birth control, Ana?"

She's silent for a moment, before she sits up and glances down at me. "That's probably not a question you want to ask right now."

CHAPTER THIRTY-FIVE

LUKE

For just a moment, I lay there, letting Ana's response sink in. She's not on birth control. It's as if someone just slammed cymbals right beside my head, the impact jolting me and then humming a bit. She might be pregnant. I wait for my rejection and panic over the idea, but I find neither of these things. In fact, the idea sits pretty well, sliding down low in my gut, and singing a bit.

I sit up next to her, intending to feel out what she's thinking, intrigued by the idea, despite the breakup convincing me a family wasn't for me. I'm shifting back into "us" mode. I hope like hell she's doing the same. We've always tended to have these shifts together, which is a shared chemistry you don't even realize as the treasure it is until you lose that treasure. Now I value everything about us a hundred times more, and I already loved the hell out of this woman. "That's a no," I say. "You are not on birth control."

"No," she says. "I'm not. I mean I brought it up, and we blew it off, and I guess I just thought—well, it's you and—"

I lean in and kiss her. "We'll name her Ashley, after your mother."

Her eyes go wide and she twists around to face me, holding onto her blanket for dear life it seems. "I'm not pregnant and we don't want kids."

"Life and death have a way of changing minds, baby. If you're pregnant, we'll embrace it."

"I don't know, Luke. A lot has changed. Everyone keeps dying. We live dangerous lives. How would we even keep a child safe?"

"Oh, we'd keep our kid safe, baby. You can count on it."

"You really want a baby?"

"Do I contemplate life and children? Not since we fell apart. Would I love the hell out of our child? Yes. Don't think that if you end up pregnant, I'm going to do anything but celebrate with you. I hope you will, too. This is not a bad thing to me. But if you're not pregnant, then we'll get birth control and revisit the idea at the right time."

"I—well—yeah," she says. "Okay. I mean the things happening right now, make me want to make a change in my life anyway."

"Meaning what?"

"I don't know yet. I guess you can help me figure that out. Tell me about your life," she says. "Where do you live?"

"Wherever you live."

"I'm serious. You have a life and a job."

"I live in New York City, but I can work and live wherever I want to. And I don't even have to do this kind of work, Ana. If we want to start a family, I've made a lot of money. More with Walker than I ever made on my own. We can get that ranch and your horses, find a place away from here and safe."

"Jake tried that. It didn't work."

"Jake made the mistake of running instead of tying up loose ends. We aren't going to do that. Speaking of," I add, and in what feels so damn surreal of a moment, I slide closer to her, cup her face and tilt her gaze to mine. I want to look into her eyes when I say this. "I don't have a new ring to give you, but I'll get one hell of a new one, Ana. Marry me. This time, let's really make it happen."

Emotions roll over her face. "God. Is this really happening? Just days ago I thought I'd never see you again. And I like the ring you gave me and I still have it."

I arch a brow. "Is that a yes?"

"Do you really even have to ask? Of course, it's a yes." Her hands press to my face. "And somewhere else, like New York even, or Montana, or Germany or wherever sounds pretty good. I think I want to sell the ranch."

I brush her hair behind her ear. "Give that some time, baby. You're reacting to what Darius told you and he really told you nothing about Kurt. Let's just see where all of this takes us."

"I don't think it's going to be a good place, Luke."

"Good, bad, or ugly, baby, we'll figure it out. Okay?"

"I think we might have to shoot some people to figure it out."

"Hey, I'm up for it. You?"

"Oh yes, I am."

"Well then, let's eat our gourmet dinner of protein bars. We're going to need our strength."

She laughs and we end up on the floor, lost in conversation, just remembering us but I realize at one point in the conversation why a baby is so damn appealing. Ana has experienced so much death and so have I, for that matter. For once, she needs to experience life. We both do.

CHAPTER THIRTY-SIX

ANA

It's early afternoon when the sun turns the snow into mush and water drips from the cabin roof and rolls down a hill in a slop of mud. When we finally pack up and load up in the SUV, with Luke behind the wheel, and me riding shotgun, it's actually with a bit of regret on my part. Once I just let go of what was happening in the rest of the world, I finally understood this little escape with Luke was necessary.

Of course, we've gone through all the evidence Darius left behind, but much of it won't mean anything until we have data access we don't have with no internet or phone. But I'm ready with pictures of everything to transmit to Blake, as soon as it's possible.

"You know what we never talked about," Luke says, when we're about halfway back to civilization.

"What?"

"The money Darius left you."

"Oh. That. Kind of weird that my dirty partner left me ten million dollars and my stepfather seems to have left me nothing."

"You inherit in a couple of years."

"I don't think there's any money. I think Kasey got it all, didn't tell me, and lost it all somehow. Probably gambling."

"Or it's more complicated than that," he says. "We both know there were things going on we don't understand. The money may have been stolen."

"The money," I say. "We don't even know there was money, really. Maybe it was Kurt who got into some kind of trouble and lost his ass. I've certainly considered that, but you know, not for long. The money never mattered to me."

"Well, we have plenty of money, baby. You're not going to want for anything."

My heart warms with his words. "I appreciate that, but all I want is you."

"And a couple of horses?"

I smile. "I really do want horses. You know I love to ride."

"Then horses you will have. Check the internet. We should be close enough by now."

I check my phone and shake my head, but then the internet pops into view. "Scratch that. We are live, Houston."

"I'll call Blake. You send that compressed photo file we made to Blake."

Luke punches in his auto-dial for Blake and allows it to ring on speaker phone. Blake answers on ring one, "Thank fuck, man. We thought you were dead. Where the hell are you?"

"It freaking snowed up in the mountains. We were trapped and had no service."

"We found the insurance Darius kept," I chime in. "I'm sending you photos but there is also audio, a lot of audio. We dictated what Darius says in his audio and I'm emailing that to you, as well."

"All right," he says. "But I have news."

My stomach knots with something in his tone. "What news?"

"Your boss is dead. He died in, get this—a car accident, just like Trevor."

I sit back with a whoosh of air exploding from my lungs and glance at Luke. "And my mother," I say, but that was when I was a kid. I don't think it was a part of this but," I swallow hard and look at Luke, "it was murder. Kurt said he made them pay."

Luke catches my hand. "Kurt didn't leave loose ends, but it's a strange coincidence. Blake—"

"I'll check it out," he confirms. "Do we have any idea what put Mike on the wrong radar?"

"Mike was the front man to whatever this operation is. It's all in the data we're transmitting. Somehow, they know we were onto him."

"You should have that data now," I say, trying to shake the whole thing about my mother off. Her death is not related to this and I've long ago dealt with her being caught in the crossfire of Kurt's enemies. It's why Kurt trained me. It's why he pushed me. "It shows delivered, Blake" I add.

The sound of a keyboard clicking under the press of fingers fills the air, and then Blake says, "Got it. Keep talking."

"They, whoever the fuck *they* are, seems to know we're onto them. They're going to clean this up and make it disappear the way Kurt's history disappeared if we don't act fast. We need you to have the team start working that data like ten minutes ago."

"We need to get to someone who knows something worth knowing before they end up dead, too." I look at Luke. "The buyer who was supposed to get that package Kasey was handling." I don't have to unzip the bag Darius left. The name is easy to remember. "Newman Phillips," I say. "Can you find him for us?"

"As in the billionaire's son?" Blake asks.

Newman being the son of Michael Phillips and everyone in Denver knows Michael. He's the owner of a Denver-based professional sports team.

"Yes," I say. "Him. Whatever these packages were that Kasey was handling, they seem to attract a lot of wealthy players."

"Give me a minute," Blake says, and he literally means a minute. The keyboard sounds start again and in just about sixty seconds exactly he says, "I'm texting you an address. Right now, he's at the stadium."

"We're a good hour and a half out from there," Luke says. "Can we get eyes on him?"

"Yeah," Blake confirms. "We'll get eyes on him. Now let me go dive into the data you sent me. And glad you're both okay. Don't go fucking around in the mountains again. I don't like that shit." Without preamble, Blake disconnects.

I glance and Luke and we laugh. "I'm thinking he meant that literally."

"Pretty accurate," he jokes.

But the lightness of the mood fades quickly for us both. "That whole car accident thing is weird, right?"

"You mean because of your mother?"

"Yes, but that was decades ago. This can't track that far back, can it?"

"I've learned to never say never. How do you feel about that?"

"I'll feel something about it later, after we kick some ass." She moves on, obviously shoving her emotions into that empty place that allows her to work. "Mike's dead. How did they figure out we knew?"

"As Darius said, they've been watching you a long time, Ana. When you showed up right after Darius died, digging around his desk, someone decided it's time to go off-grid for a while. And when you go off-grid, you cut off the head of the snake that can bite you."

He's right. And my fear is they aren't done finding those snakes and killing them. If they get to the sources of information before we do, we'll never figure this out.

"I assume Mike was behind the meetup we were supposed to have at the ranch," Luke says. "If he's dead, the question is, who is in charge and who, if anyone, is showing up to that meeting?"

Who indeed, I think, and why does that question twist me in knots?

CHAPTER THIRTY-SEVEN

LUKE

By the time we're back within the Denver city limits, Newman Phillips has left the stadium and gone to his luxury home on Polo Club Lane. We arrive at a security gate that Blake opens remotely for us. We travel a long circle drive with a bunch of sharply cut bushes to part at the foot of a long stairwell. Ana and I both have our weapons easily accessible as we ring the bell. No one answers. We ring again.

My phone rings with Blake's number and I answer on speaker. "You're sure he's here?"

"He's there, but there's a weird as fuck formation to his security feed. I have a bad feeling about this. Go in."

"Happy to please, boss," I say, disconnecting and scanning the property. "Let's look for a back entrance."

Ana nods, we draw our weapons, and split up. I go left. She goes right. We come together at the rear garage where the door is open.

"Damn it," Ana murmurs, because we both know what we're about to find.

We ease forward into the garage, Ana on the passenger side, me on the driver's side. "Fuck," I murmur.

Newman's brains are splattered all over the window. He's dead.

Ana joins me, takes one look, and groans. "Damn it." But she also immediately kicks into agent mode, lifting her chin toward the house. "Let's hope the asshole who did this is still here. Someone needs to talk to us."

Fifteen minutes later, Blake takes over the law enforcement side of things and tells us to get the hell out of the line of fire. Once Ana and I are on the road, I make an executive decision. "They're coming for us, baby. We need to go where we have the best chance of winning."

"The Ranch," she says.

"Yes. The Ranch. Agreed?"

"Agreed."

"I'll have Savage and Adam meet us there."

"And Parker?" she queries.

"Right. And Parker."

She laughs. "You really turned sour on him."

"He's alive," I say. "If I'd soured on him, and he was involved in all of this, he'd be dead."

CHAPTER THIRTY-EIGHT

ANA

We bring The Ranch into view and I swear I feel it like a punch in the chest, the way I did right after Kurt died. Everything feels unsettling where Kurt comes into play. Everything I thought I knew I no longer believe I know at all. Nothing is as it seems. Who knew just how real those words would become. Luke and I are not over, for starters. In fact, we're engaged again. That alone is one of the wonders of the world.

If only everything I thought I knew, but didn't know, translated to something as wonderful as finding Luke again.

But it doesn't and outside of the Darius revelations, there are more coming. Soon. Really soon. I feel it in my bones.

Luke drives us through the gate openings to the property which is miles and miles of land, all of which is a mock battlefield, complete with hidden tunnels, booby traps, and mind games. Kurt was always so good at mind games. He played them with me from the time I was a young girl. I know first-hand that this is a place that makes boys into men and men into warriors and in some cases, monsters. They also made a little girl who loved Barbie dolls into an FBI agent.

The central property, which was Kurt's home, allows for public entry. A necessity considering the training operation this place housed.

"We won't have garage access," I tell him.

"I'll pull to the rear and after we ensure the house is clear, we'll pull it into the garage out of sight."

I nod, that twisty feeling in my belly tightening a bit more. I hate being here today, when this place should be empowering. I know it as I know my own name. Intimately, automatically, perfectly. Luke pulls us to the rear of the house, as the rental doesn't have a connection to the garage, with plans to hide our presence by moving the vehicle later.

Luke's phone rings and he answers with, "Where are you?" then glances in his rearview.

I turn to find another SUV headed our way. *The rest of our team*, I think.

"Pull to the rear," Luke informs them, confirming their identity.

Once we're parked, Luke and I head to the door. I unlock it and we step inside and my gut goes wild. I instantly know something is wrong. Or maybe this place just feels wrong to me now, because I don't know the man who once lived here. He had secrets. I'm not sure what to think about just how deeply they seemed to run. Luke walks toward the kitchen to clear the property. I am drawn to Kurt's office, almost as if a magnetic field drags me in that direction. I step to the center of the double doors and my breath hitches.

Kurt is sitting at the desk.

He stands up, tall, and healthy looking, his body fit, his face full, but still chiseled. Almost as if he's been on a really good vacation.

"Ana," he says. "It's been too long." He rounds the desk and steps in front of me, and I can see the green of his eyes, with the little orange flecks that reminded the sixteen-year-old me of the fires of hell when he was screaming training commands at me.

I stand there, stunned, unable to move, my feet planted to the ground as if the carpet were cement. "How are you here? What is this?"

"What the fuck, Kurt?" Luke demands, stepping to my side.

I'm remotely aware of a door opening. Of footsteps behind the three of us, and I want to shout for them to leave, to allow us time to process and claim the answers we deserve. That *I* deserve.

"Everything is not what it seems," Kurt says. "It's a lot worse, Ana."

"What does that mean?" I demand, my voice trembling, while Luke's possessive, protective energy pops beside me.

"Start talking, Kurt," Luke demands tightly, and it's really not a shock when he draws on him, aiming his weapon at him, "because I haven't decided if I should be celebrating right now or shooting you."

Suddenly the dynamic changes. Another person enters the picture. "Kurt, you bastard. You really need to just die already, but at least I can finally make you pay properly for your stupidity."

I whirl around to find Parker holding a gun over my head, pointing it at Kurt. Adam and Savage are not here, at least not in this moment, and I don't know why. I can barely process what is happening. Why is Parker here and they are not? I never get a chance to ask. The next thing I know I'm grabbed from behind and Kurt has a hold of me, with a gun pointed at my head.

He eyes Luke and issues a command. *"Kill him."*

I'm his shelter because he fears Luke will kill him. And I think he might have to.

My fiancé was forced to kill my brother. Now I think he might be forced to kill the only man I've ever really looked at as a father.

THE END...FOR NOW

***

LUKE AND ANA RETURN VERY SOON!

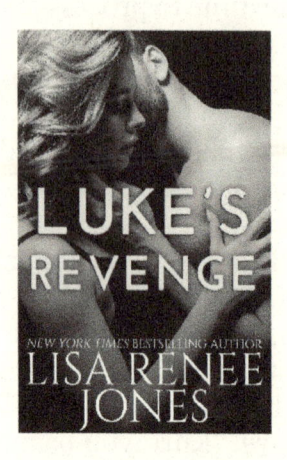

In the mind-blowing and stunning finale, all will be revealed as Luke's forever with the woman he loves hangs in the balance.

PRE-ORDER THE FINALE HERE
https://www.lisareneejones.com/walker-security-lucifers-trilogy.html

***

WANT A CHANCE TO READ TYLER & BELLA'S DUET BEFORE ANYONE ELSE? SIGN-UP BELOW!

Tyler Hawk is a man with secrets and a dark past. A man who has known tragedy and betrayal. He wants for little, but what he wants is more power, a legacy that is his own, and not his father's. There are obstacles in his way, one of which is the scandal his father left behind and a will with certain demands.

Behind the scenes he is a man on edge, and only one woman sees the truth hidden beneath his strong will and dominant rule. Bella is somehow demanding and submissive, fiery and yet sweet. She can give him everything he wants, she just doesn't know it, not yet, but she will. If she'll just say yes and sign on the dotted line.

SIGN-UP FOR THE CHANCE TO WIN AN ARC:
https://www.subscribepage.com/tylerbellaarc

PRE-ORDER THE DUET HERE:

https://www.lisareneejones.com/tyler--bella-duet.html

***

AND DON'T MISS THE NEXT BOOK IN THE LILAH LOVE SERIES—HAPPY DEATH DAY!

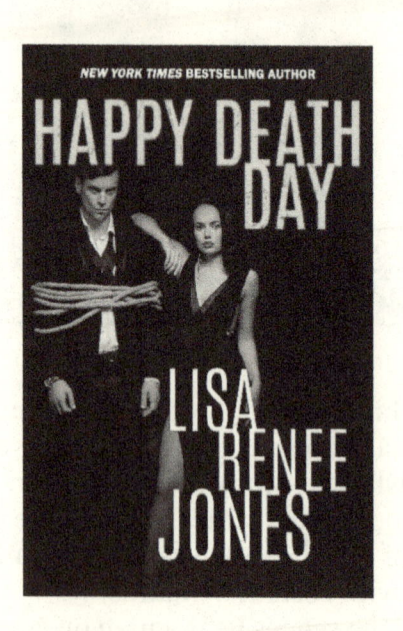

Kane Mendez.

The son of a drug lord, who is not his father's son, and yet, he has enemies. Too many enemies.

Lilah Love.

The FBI agent who perhaps kills a little too easily. Or does she? As she's called in to consult on a case, and catch a killer, her troubles back home don't go away. People want her dead. She simply wants them dead first.

Kane and Lilah. Lilah and Kane. War is on the horizon. And everyone won't survive.

FIND OUT MORE ABOUT HAPPY DEATH DAY HERE:
https://www.lisareneejonesthrillers.com/the-lilah-love-series.html#HappyDeathDay

***

Don't forget, if you want to be the first to know about upcoming books, giveaways, sales, and any other exciting news I have to share please be sure you're signed up for my newsletter! As an added bonus everyone receives a free eBook when they sign-up!

http://lisareneejones.com/newsletter-sign-up/

BE THE FIRST TO KNOW!

THE BEST WAY TO BE INFORMED OF ALL UPCOMING BOOKS, SALES, GIVEAWAYS, AND TO GET A FREE EBOOK, BE SURE YOU'RE SIGNED UP FOR MY NEWSLETTER LIST!

SIGN-UP HERE:
http://lisareneejones.com/newsletter-sign-up/

ANOTHER SUREFIRE WAY TO BE IN THE KNOW IS TO FOLLOW ME ON SOCIAL MEDIA:

Facebook: https://www.facebook.com/AuthorLisaReneeJones/
Facebook Group: https://www.facebook.com/groups/LRJbooks
Instagram: https://www.instagram.com/lisareneejones/
TikTok: https://www.tiktok.com/@lisareneejonesbooks
Twitter: http://www.twitter.com/LisaReneeJones
BookBub: https://www.bookbub.com/authors/lisa-renee-jones

THE NECKLACE TRILOGY

A necklace delivered to the wrong Allison: me. I'm the wrong Allison.

That misplaced gift places a man in my path. A man who instantly consumes me and leads me down a path of dark secrets and intense passion.

Dash Black is a famous, bestselling author, but also a man born into wealth and power. He owns everything around him, every room he enters. He owns me the moment I meet him. He seduces me oh so easily and reveals another side of myself I dared not expose. Until him. Until this intense, wonderful, tormented man shows me another way to live and love. I melt when he kisses me. I shiver when he touches me. And I like when he's in control, especially when I thought I'd never allow anyone that much power over me ever again.

We are two broken people who are somehow whole when we are together, but those secrets—his, and yes, I have mine as well—threaten to shatter all that is right and make it wrong.

FIND OUT MORE ABOUT THE NECKLACE TRILOGY HERE:
https://www.lisareneejones.com/necklace-trilogy.html

ALSO BY LISA RENEE JONES

THE INSIDE OUT SERIES

If I Were You
Being Me
Revealing Us
*His Secrets**
Rebecca's Lost Journals
*The Master Undone**
*My Hunger**
No In Between
*My Control**
I Belong to You
*All of Me**

THE SECRET LIFE OF AMY BENSEN

Escaping Reality
Infinite Possibilities
Forsaken
*Unbroken**

CARELESS WHISPERS

Denial
Demand
Surrender

WHITE LIES

Provocative
Shameless

TALL, DARK & DEADLY / WALKER SECURITY

Hot Secrets
Dangerous Secrets
Beneath the Secrets
Deep Under
Pulled Under
Falling Under
Savage Hunger
Savage Burn
Savage Love
Savage Ending
When He's Dirty
When He's Bad
When He's Wild

LILAH LOVE

Murder Notes
Murder Girl
Love Me Dead
Love Kills
Bloody Vows
Bloody Love
Happy Death Day
The Party's Over

DIRTY RICH

Dirty Rich One Night Stand
Dirty Rich Cinderella Story
Dirty Rich Obsession
Dirty Rich Betrayal
Dirty Rich Cinderella Story: Ever After
Dirty Rich One Night Stand: Two Years Later
Dirty Rich Obsession: All Mine
Dirty Rich Secrets
Dirty Rich Betrayal: Love Me Forever

THE FILTHY TRILOGY

The Bastard
The Princess
The Empire

THE NAKED TRILOGY

One Man
One Woman
Two Together

THE BRILLIANCE TRILOGY

A Reckless Note
A Wicked Song
A Sinful Encore

NECKLACE TRILOGY

What If I Never

Because I Can
When I Say Yes

LUCIFER'S TRILOGY

Luke's Sin
Luke's Touch
Luke's Revenge

*eBook only

ABOUT LISA RENEE JONES

New York Times and USA Today bestselling author Lisa Renee Jones writes dark, edgy fiction including the highly acclaimed *Inside Out* series and the crime thriller *The Poet*. Suzanne Todd (producer of Alice in Wonderland and Bad Moms) on the *Inside Out* series: *Lisa has created a beautiful, complicated, and sensual world that is filled with intrigue and suspense.*

Prior to publishing, Lisa owned a multi-state staffing agency that was recognized many times by The Austin Business Journal and also praised by the Dallas Women's Magazine. In 1998 Lisa was listed as the #7 growing women-owned business in Entrepreneur Magazine. She lives in Colorado with her husband, a cat that talks too much, and a Golden Retriever who is afraid of trash bags.

Made in the USA
Coppell, TX
07 July 2022

79677192R00122